Best Family Ever

Also by **Karen Kingsbury**

Inspirational Fiction for Adults

The Chance
Fifteen Minutes
The Bridge

Angels Walking Series

Angels Walking
Chasing Sunsets
Brush of Wings

The Baxter Collection

Love Story
A Baxter Family Christmas
In This Moment
When We Were Young

A **BAXTER FAMILY CHILDREN** *Story*

Best Family Ever

KAREN KINGSBURY

and TYLER RUSSELL

A Paula Wiseman Book

Simon & Schuster Books for Young Readers

NEW YORK · LONDON · TORONTO · SYDNEY · NEW DELHI

SIMON & SCHUSTER BOOKS FOR YOUNG READERS
An imprint of Simon & Schuster Children's Publishing Division
1230 Avenue of the Americas, New York, New York 10020
This book is a work of fiction. Any references to historical events, real people, or real places are used fictitiously. Other names, characters, places, and events are products of the author's imagination, and any resemblance to actual events or places or persons, living or dead, is entirely coincidental.
SIMON & SCHUSTER BOOKS FOR YOUNG READERS
is a trademark of Simon & Schuster, Inc.
For information about special discounts for bulk purchases, please contact
Simon & Schuster Special Sales at 1-866-506-1949 or business@simonandschuster.com.
The Simon & Schuster Speakers Bureau can bring authors to your live event.
For more information or to book an event, contact the Simon & Schuster Speakers Bureau
at 1-866-248-3049 or visit our website at www.simonspeakers.com.
Also available in a Simon & Schuster Books for Young Readers hardcover edition
Book design by Laurent Linn
The text for this book was set in ArrusBT Std.
Manufactured in the United States of America
1119 MTN
First Simon & Schuster Books for Young Readers paperback edition January 2020
2 4 6 8 10 9 7 5 3 1
The Library of Congress has cataloged the hardcover edition as follows:
Names: Kingsbury, Karen, author. | Russell, Tyler, author.
Title: Best family ever / Karen Kingsbury ; with Tyler Russell.
Description: First edition. | New York : Simon & Schuster Books for Young Readers,
[2019] | Series: The Baxter family children | "A Paula Wiseman Book." | Summary:
"When Dr. Baxter tells the family that they will be moving from Ann Arbor, Michigan, to
Bloomington, Indiana, the five Baxter children, ages six to thirteen, are sure that their lives
and home will never be the same. But they find that being together with the ones
you love is the most important part of home"—Provided by publisher.
Identifiers: LCCN 2018006712| ISBN 9781534412156 (hardcover : alk. paper)
ISBN 9781534412163 (pbk)| ISBN 9781534412170 (eBook)
Subjects: | CYAC: Family life—Fiction. | Brothers and sisters—Fiction. | Moving,
Household—Fiction. | Friendship—Fiction. | Home—Fiction. | Christian life—Fiction.
Classification: LCC PZ7.K6117 Be 2019 | DDC [Fic]—dc23
LC record available at https://lccn.loc.gov/2018006712

Dedicated to Donald, my Prince Charming. I love you with all my heart. You are my hero, my forever and always. Also, to my children, who were growing up when I began writing about the Baxters, and who will now read these books to their children. And to God Almighty, who continues to give me the most beautiful life with all of them.—Karen

Dedicated to you, the reader. Never stop chasing your dreams. Remember, there is only one you! Also to my family—you are the reason for so many of the stories in these pages, and you inspire me in countless ways. Thank you for the memories, the friendship, and for always making me better. I love you. And finally to my Lord and Savior, Jesus Christ. This is because of You and all for You. May You be glorified in all I do.—Tyler

Best Family Ever

Meet the Baxter Family

Dear Reader,

In the most wonderful way, the Baxter family has become one of the world's most beloved fictional families. I began writing about Dr. John Baxter; his wife, Elizabeth; and their adult children when my own children were growing up. All told there are dozens of books in the adult Baxter family series. I'm still writing adult books about the Baxters.

But recently I began to think about you. My younger reader. And I wondered what would happen if I journeyed back to the beginning of the Baxter family. Back to when the Baxter children were young. Suddenly my heart was filled with dozens of stories yet untold.

This is one of those.

And here's the fun part. I'm writing the Baxter Family Children books with Tyler Russell, my oldest son. One of the kids who sat around my dinner table when the Baxters first took root in my heart.

For the purposes of this first Baxter Family Children book, here are the Baxter children:

BROOKE BAXTER, 13—a seventh grader at Kennedy Middle School in Ann Arbor, Michigan. She is studious and smart. She has her own room.

KARI BAXTER, 11—a fifth grader at Johnson Elementary School. She is beautiful, kind and careful. She shares a room with Ashley.

ASHLEY BAXTER, 10—a fourth grader at Johnson Elementary. She looks like Kari, and she loves sports. But she definitely feels misunderstood.

ERIN BAXTER, 8—a second grader at Johnson Elementary. She is quiet and soft-spoken, and she loves being with their mom. She shares a room with Luke.

LUKE BAXTER, 6—a first grader at Johnson Elementary. He's good at sports, hyper and happy. He loves God and his family, especially Ashley.

1

Winter

ASHLEY

Fourth grade at Johnson Elementary School was turning out to be Ashley Baxter's best year ever. This week in Miss Wilson's class they were studying snowflakes. Beautiful creative snowflakes, of all things!

And it was even supposed to snow today.

Ashley twirled off the school bus and danced on her tiptoes, eyes fixed on the gray sky, her arms stretched wide. This was how a snowflake might feel. Ashley was pretty sure, because a snowflake spent its entire life dancing through space.

Her goal was to twirl all the way to her classroom. But Ashley must have lost track of where she was going, or which way she was turning, because all the sudden she heard a yelling voice.

"Watch out, Baxter!" The words were from a boy and they sounded mean.

Before Ashley could figure out who they were coming from, someone crashed into her.

A strange sound came from her lips, like the air was leaving her lungs all at once.

She couldn't even get a deep breath before she and the boy fell to the ground. From the corner of her eye, Ashley saw a football roll a few feet from her. That's when she figured out who had hit her.

It was Eric Powers. Rudest boy in her class.

"Why were you spinning?" Eric made a face at her. Four other kids walked by, headed to class. Every one of them was watching.

Great, Ashley thought.

She stood and crossed her arms. "Um. It's homework. Just so you know." She stared at him, her eyes squinty. "And it's *Ashley* . . . not Baxter!"

Why did *he* have to run into her? Of all people?

"Homework? Twirling?" Eric picked up the football and stood right in front of her, the ball under his arm. Suddenly his angry face relaxed. A slow sort of smile came over him. Like they were friends. "What sort of homework?"

"If I have to explain it to you, Eric, then you really just don't get it." Ashley huffed. Eric didn't understand. The bell rang and students all over the school yard rushed inside. Ashley took one last look up at the sky and closed her eyes. *Who cares what Eric thinks*. She could pretend to be a snowflake. At least for now.

"Ashley! Time to come in." Miss Wilson peeked out from the classroom door. "It's freezing out here."

"Yes, ma'am!" Ashley ran toward the door, out of the cold and into the toasty classroom. She hung up her jacket and took a seat next to her best school friend in all the world. Lydia Christina.

"Why were you dancing out there?" Lydia didn't look away from the book she was reading. But she raised her eyebrows high above the rim of her glasses.

"I was being a snowflake." Ashley folded her hands nice and neat on her desk.

3

"Naturally." Lydia looked at her and laughed a little. "You're the silliest girl in fourth grade. That's why I like you."

"It wasn't that silly." Ashley glanced over at Miss Wilson. The teacher was walking up and down the aisles handing out papers. Which meant Ashley and Lydia could still talk for a few minutes.

"You stepped off the bus and started spinning." Lydia kept her voice quiet. "You're the only one I know who would do that."

Lydia's words felt like a compliment. Ashley smiled, more relaxed. "Aren't you going to ask me what it was like?" She leaned back in her chair. "Being a snowflake?"

"Okay. What was it like?" Lydia set her book down and looked at Ashley. "Didn't seem like it ended very well."

"It didn't." Ashley made a face. "Eric Powers bumped into me and we both crashed to the ground."

"Well . . ." Lydia angled her head. "That is sort of how it ends for snowflakes. They all pretty much float to the ground."

Ashley hadn't thought about that. "True." She

looked over at Eric, who was laughing with the other boys. Probably about her.

"Which means I will probably never play the snowflake game." Lydia pointed at the dirt on Ashley's knees. "Not before school, anyway."

"Snowflake game . . . ?" Ashley brushed her knees clean and then did the same to her elbows. She rolled her eyes. Lydia didn't understand, either. For everything she had in common with her friend, there were some things where they were complete and total opposites.

Be patient, Ashley reminded herself. Not out loud, but inside her head. Her mom said she should work on patience. So this was her chance to practice. "Lydia." Ashley used her kindest voice. "It wasn't a snowflake game. It was homework."

"Homework?" Lydia scrunched up her face, like she was confused.

"Miss Wilson said, remember? She asked us to think what it might be like being a snowflake."

"Right. Okay." Lydia picked up her book and found her page. "You're a funny one, Ashley Baxter."

Ashley blinked a few times. Whatever. Lydia thought she was silly, but Ashley didn't mind. They would always be friends. Forever and ever. "How about we both pretend to be snowflakes at recess?"

Lydia looked up from her book, her eyes sparkly. "It did sort of look fun."

They were both giggling when Miss Wilson walked to the front of the classroom. "All right. Settle down." She waited for everyone to sit. Then she smiled at them. "Good news, boys and girls. Next week is a special day. Who knows what it is?"

Lydia's hand went up first. "Valentine's Day. A day where we celebrate St. Valentine and friendship."

"And get lots of candy," Eric blurted out from the back of the classroom. A few of the boys around him laughed again.

There he goes. Ashley shook her head. *That boy thinks he's so funny.*

Miss Wilson took a step closer. "You are both right. So later today we are going to discuss St. Valentine and the history of Valentine's Day!" Miss Wilson pointed to the nearest desk. "I just gave you an activity sheet, so we can talk about this holiday together."

Ashley looked out the window. She wasn't the biggest fan of Valentine's Day. She never got the most valentine cards. Everyone was supposed to give one to every boy and girl. But she always felt like the other kids got more. She'd rather study snowflakes.

Then, while she was still looking outside, the most amazing thing happened! The smallest, softest, most delicate snowflakes began to fall to the ground. Just like the ones she was pretending to be when she climbed off the bus.

How would that feel, being a real snowflake? Dancing and twirling and drifting down from heaven? Out of nowhere she felt Lydia give her a jab in her side. "Ouch." Ashley turned to her friend. "That hurt!"

"Ashley!" Lydia pointed to the front of the class. "Miss Wilson asked you a question."

In a rush, Ashley looked at their teacher, whose eyes were definitely watching her. Ashley let out a little laugh and smiled. "Sorry."

"Ashley. Please stay with us." Miss Wilson put her hands on her hips. "I asked the class to find a reason to use the word *effervescent* today. Do you know what that means?"

The whole class was watching her. The word was on her spelling list. She tapped her desk. "Bubbly?"

Miss Wilson nodded. "Yes. Bubbly and enthusiastic." She smiled. "And even though you, yourself, are effervescent, I still need you to focus."

"I'm trying."

"Try harder." Miss Wilson's look was serious.

Suddenly Ashley thought of something to explain herself. "Well, the truth is . . ." A quick bunch of words filled Ashley's head. They were out before she could stop them. "I was so focused on your snowflake teaching from yesterday . . . and then I looked outside and saw the beautiful snow. And I thought, *Wouldn't it be great if we could all learn our spelling words* outside?"

"In the snow?" Miss Wilson leaned against her desk. She blew at a piece of her hair and shook her head.

"It hasn't snowed since last week." Ashley

blinked. "Outside would be perfect. Don't you guys think so?" She looked around the room. But she was met with absolute silence. Clearly no one was with her on this.

Eric Powers whispered loud enough for Ashley to hear. "Crazy Baxter."

Their teacher didn't hear him. She was still standing in front of Ashley. She didn't look too thrilled.

Lydia shook her head and stared down at her desk.

"I appreciate your creativity, Ashley. But I think everyone else would like to have the lesson *inside*." Miss Wilson turned to the blackboard.

Ashley slouched in her chair and tried to pay attention. She'd already been in trouble twice this month for not paying attention. But sometimes she couldn't help it. All day long the edges of her mind spilled over with extra thoughts.

This wasn't turning out to be a very good day. Miss Wilson reprimanding her in front of the whole class, and the fact that no one else wanted to go outside.

Recess wasn't much better. Lydia tried to be a

snowflake, but she got dizzy and fell in the snow. Only it was actually not very much snow. More like mud. So Lydia's hair got streaked with wet dirt.

At the end of the day, when the bell rang, Lydia gave Ashley a look. "I almost forgot!" She stuffed her notebook into her backpack. "Why did you ask to have class outside? Miss Wilson was never going to say yes to that."

"Are you serious?" Ashley's mouth hung open for a few seconds. "That was a great idea! Learning in the snow? Can you imagine?"

"No." Lydia made her eyes wide. "Now Miss Wilson is going to call your mom and you're going to be in trouble. Because you don't pay attention." Lydia shook her head. "And who wants to study in the snow, anyway? Too cold, if you ask me."

"Lydia." Ashley stared at her. "You're my best school friend. And I would do anything for you. But sometimes I don't get you." Ashley grabbed her things. *If only Lydia wasn't so sensible.*

So they could be snowflakes together—even in the mud.

On the way out of the classroom, Ashley stopped

at Miss Wilson's desk. Then she turned to Lydia. She gripped the straps of her backpack and used her most quiet voice. "I'll meet you in the hall."

"Okay." Lydia looked worried as she hurried out of the classroom.

Alone with Miss Wilson, Ashley rocked back and forth on her toes. "So . . ." She smiled. "Am I in trouble?"

Miss Wilson looked up from her papers. "No, Ashley. You mean well. I see that." The teacher's smile looked tired. "And I'm not going to call your mom. But you need to pay attention in class." She raised her brow. "Do you understand?"

"Yes!" Ashley's heart felt light as a snowflake. She wasn't in trouble! "Yes, I understand." She ran around to the other side of the desk and gave Miss Wilson a quick hug. "Thank you, thank you, thank you!" She could barely contain herself. "I'll do better, I promise."

Miss Wilson's eyes sparkled. "Now. What would you think about being in charge of our Valentine's Day party?"

"Me?" Ashley couldn't believe it. Miss Wilson

had never asked her to be in charge of anything this important. "Really?"

"Yes." A quiet laugh came from Miss Wilson. "Out of the whole class, I figured you'd be the one to make our party just right." Miss Wilson smiled at her. "No one is more . . . effervescent."

Ashley glowed under that compliment. She gave Miss Wilson another hug. "Can Lydia help?"

Miss Wilson laughed again. "Of course. Let me know what you girls need." She pointed to the door. "The bus is waiting. See you tomorrow."

"This is the best news." Ashley practically danced to the door. "I already have a thousand ideas. You won't be disappointed . . . I promise."

Once she was out of the classroom, Ashley bolted down the hall and caught up to Lydia. She shared the whole story with her, and they talked about how they were going to plan the best party ever. "Party planners extraordinaire." Ashley danced down the hall. Like she was a model on a runway.

"Look out, here we come." Lydia giggled as she joined in.

"Can you picture it?" Ashley twirled. "Snowflakes and hearts everywhere. And streamers."

Lydia gave her a look. "Not snowflakes again, Ashley."

"Fine. I can give up the snowflakes." Ashley skipped down the steps of the school. "Do you think we need some pink?"

"Definitely!" Lydia got louder now, more excited. "Everything needs to be pink. And red and white!"

"Exactly." Ashley's heart beat faster because of pure joy. This was going to be the best party any fourth-grade class ever had.

When they reached the bus, Lydia headed for her mom's car. "Talk to you tomorrow."

"Perfect." Ashley still couldn't believe it. She was in charge of the Valentine's Day party! Ashley practically floated down the sidewalk. A quick turn around the brick building and there they were! Her siblings, already getting on the bus.

Kari and Erin, and Luke. Her other best friends. Her *very* best friends.

She could hardly wait to tell them the news.

2

Best Family Ever

ASHLEY

Ashley ran to the bus, and as she did she could hear her mother's voice in her memory. The sound of it made her feel loved.

Your very best friends are the ones around the dinner table each night. Her mom always smiled when she said that. And then she would say, *Many years from now, even when everything seems like it has changed, you'll still have each other.*

Every time their mom said that, a warm feeling spread through Ashley's heart. Because it was true. The Baxter children were the best of friends.

"Hurry, Ash!" Kari stood on the top step of the bus and reached out her hand. "It's freezing!"

Ashley took her sister's hand and stepped onto the bus. She was the last to board, so the driver closed the door and they headed off. Like always, Ashley sat next to Kari. The two were kindred spirits. Like Anne and Diana from *Anne of Green Gables*. Kari was eleven, and Ashley was only a year younger. Like twins, almost. They shared a room, too.

So of course they were the closest.

Brooke was the oldest. She was thirteen and at Kennedy Middle School this year. They wouldn't see Brooke until they were home. In front of Ashley and Kari sat their youngest two siblings. Erin, who was eight, and Luke, who had just turned six.

Erin and Luke shared a room, too, but Ashley could never understand how that worked out. Erin was the quietest kid in the family and Luke was the loudest. Their mom said it was all about balance.

Whatever that meant.

Even now Erin had a book open before the bus pulled away from the front of the school.

"What are you reading?" Ashley leaned forward, her knees pressed into the seat, so she could see Erin. Her sister had the prettiest light blond hair.

"Charlotte's Web." Erin turned around and gave Ashley a thumbs-up. "I'm at the best part. When Wilbur tries to spin like a spider!" Ashley nodded. She hadn't read it. No time. She would get the summary from Erin later.

Next to Erin, Luke was bouncing in his seat. Without warning he started singing. "Old McDonald had a farm, E-I-E-I-O . . . and on that farm he had a cow . . ."

Ashley sat back and shared a soft laugh with Kari. Luke was always singing. Especially songs with sounds.

But now Luke was mooing. And everyone on the bus was turning to look at him.

Ashley put her face close to Kari's. "He's a pretty good cow. Realistic," she whispered.

"True." They both giggled. Then Kari tapped their brother's shoulder. "Luke, buddy, maybe not so loud."

"It's better loud!" Luke grinned over his shoulder and kept singing. "And on that farm he had a chicken . . . E-I-E-I-O."

Ashley liked his spunk. He was effervescent,

16

just like her. When the song ended, Ashley put her hand on his shoulder. "Did you play basketball at recess?"

"Yep." Luke was waiting for two new teeth to come in. Ashley thought he looked cute. Luke grinned. "I scored three times. Wanna know something else?"

"Sure." Ashley loved her little brother. "What?"

"We started learning to write the alphabet today." Luke pulled out his notebook and opened the pages. He laughed as he looked at his work. "Mine wasn't the best."

Ashley studied the page. Nothing there looked like the alphabet. At least not the English alphabet. "I think it's perfect." She smiled. "I'm proud of you!"

"Thanks." Luke grinned. Just then his friend across the aisle started talking about dinosaurs, so Ashley leaned back in her seat and turned to Kari. Her older sister was quiet, staring out the window. Ashley tapped her shoulder. "What're you thinking about?"

Kari's eyes were soft when she turned to Ashley.

Her voice, too. "Dreams." She looked like her thoughts were far away. "You know, like being a grown-up." Kari thought for a minute. "Ashley, when you think about the future, where do you think you'll be?"

"Oh wow. Now *that's* a big question. I'm not sure." Ashley puffed her cheeks big, and blew the air out, dramatic. Then all at once the answer came to her. "Actually I do know. I'll be a professional soccer player . . . and a painter. And I'll be so good at painting that I'll move to Paris, where the famous artists live."

Ashley stopped for a breath. "Remember Paris? Dad told us about it last week at dinner. He and Mom want to take us there sometime. You know, the pretty buildings . . . the river. The Awful Tower. Paris is right by London, where the Queen lives."

"The Awful Tower?" Kari didn't seem to be following.

"Yes." Ashley rolled her eyes. "It's famous. Everyone knows about it." Ashley could see her grown-up days like they were happening right now. "And after that I'll have lots of kids like Mom and

18

Dad and I'll be a cook so I can make them dinner." Ashley laughed. "Yes, I can definitely see it. Soccer. Paris. Family. All that." She thought for a few seconds. It was possible, right? She lifted her shoulders a few times. "What about you?"

"Wait. So you're moving to Paris?" Kari looked horrified, like the time when she had come home from a weekend at her friend Sarah Grace's house to find a million fall leaves spread out over their bedroom floor.

Ashley had only been doing a little fall decorating. Mom had made her clean the room, of course. Every leaf. And looking back, Ashley had to admit that it hadn't been her best idea. But the thing Ashley remembered most was the shocked look on Kari's face.

It had looked like her sister was going to faint.

Which was exactly how Kari looked now. Plus she looked very sad about Ashley moving to Paris and being so far away. "Don't worry, Kari." Ashley patted her sister's hand. "I won't be gone very long." She tried to think of something encouraging. "And you can visit."

Kari looked out the window again and sighed. Finally she faced Ashley. "I think growing up is going to be hard." She paused. "We had an assignment today, to make a collage of dreams. I guess I never really think much about it."

"A collage of dreams." Ashley smiled. "I like that."

"I guess." Kari looked at her again. "I don't know my dreams yet."

"Okay." Ashley faced her sister. "Let's say you could do anything in the whole world. What would you do?" Ashley waited. "That's what should go on a collage of dreams."

"Hmm." Kari waited a few breaths. "I want to help people, I guess. And have a family like ours."

Ashley bit the inside of her cheek. Kari's idea was nice, but not really like a dream. She had an idea. Something that she knew would help. "Maybe you should talk to God about your dreams." It was something their mother would've said. "God will help you figure it out."

The bus pulled up to their stop, and Ashley and her siblings got out. The snow crunched under their boots as they headed for home. On the way, they spotted something that made them all stop in their tracks. A big yellow moving truck was parked in their neighbors' driveway.

The house looked empty and sad.

Ashley's stomach started to hurt. "The Johnsons are moving?" She stared at the truck. The Johnsons had lived there forever.

"Mom said that Mrs. Johnson got a job in California." Kari's breath hung in the freezing air.

Ashley couldn't believe it. "But school just started up again . . ."

"I'm never moving." Erin took Luke's hand. "Not ever."

"Me, too." Kari looked back at the truck once more as the four of them started walking again.

Ashley thought of something. "I'm glad our dad has a job right here. Because I'm never moving, either."

Kari looked at her. "I thought you were moving to Paris."

"I changed my mind." Ashley thought about

her family, the best family, the Baxter family, and how hard it would be to leave here. Nowhere in the world would be as good as Ann Arbor.

Not ever.

Kari must have known what was on Ashley's mind. She took her hand. "Don't worry. We aren't moving anywhere. This is our home."

They rounded the corner of their street and there, at the end of the cul-de-sac, was their house. Two stories tall, made of bricks as white as the snow. Black shutters and lights on in the windows. In the spring the trees that lined the side yard bloomed the most beautiful pink flowers in all the neighborhood. The steps to the door were brick, and a metal porch railing ran along either side. Just perfect for spiky icicles. The cobblestone driveway was prettier than anything in Paris.

It was theirs. And it was Ashley's favorite place.

The four of them walked up the steps and Ashley opened the door. As they stepped inside, the smell of warm cinnamon and brown sugar rushed to meet them.

"Snickerdoodles!" Ashley started to run to the

kitchen. She didn't need to worry about moving. The Baxter family would never leave home.

"Boots off!" Their mom's voice sounded like a smile from the kitchen. Ashley dropped to the floor, grunting as she yanked her snow boots off one at a time. She threw her bag on the floor. *Thwap!* At the same time, Kari, Erin, and Luke hung theirs on the racks bolted to the wall near the front door.

"Ashley." Her mom came around the corner, wiping her hands on her apron. Mom's eyes were friendly, but her words were definitely firm. Her do-it-now-or-else voice, Ashley called it. Her mother put her hands on her hips. "Hang your backpack please. I tell you every day." She turned and walked back to the kitchen.

Ashley opened her mouth and stared at Kari. "How does she know?"

"She *always* knows." Kari giggled.

Five minutes later they were in the kitchen, staring at their mother's fresh-baked snickerdoodles. Ashley sat on one of the barstools along the counter. "Where's Brooke?"

"Upstairs. Speech and debate competition Friday."

Her mom took another tray of cookies out of the oven, checked them and put them back in.

Ashley slumped a little. "She's always in her room."

"She's three years older than you, honey." Her mom looked straight at Ashley, the kind of look that felt like a hug. "She has to study. And she does love you."

Deep breath, Ashley told herself. "I know"—she sat a little straighter—"I love her, too." She tapped her finger on the counter. "Now . . . about that backpack."

"It belongs on the hook." Her mom returned to the plate of cookies. "Let's talk about your day. Who's ready for a snack?"

Ashley's siblings talked all at once. "We are!"

"Yes, please."

Ashley waited till they were finished. She still had a point to make. "I have to get my backpack down for homework anyway. Besides, then I leave a hook for Daddy. For his briefcase."

Her mom looked at her. The same kind of look Miss Wilson always gave. "Ashley. Your father

24

hung those hooks for you kids. Not for his briefcase. This isn't open to debate." She looked at Kari
and Luke and Erin. "Grab a napkin. Two each."

Fine. She would use the hooks. Ashley jumped
up and grabbed a pair of snickerdoodles. She took
extra time picking the supersoft ones.

"Luke, stay away from the batter." Their mother
spun around and looked at Luke. He was in the
corner, fingers covered in dough. "Where are your
cookies?"

"I ate 'em." Luke was always hungry. "The
dough's so good, Mommy. Please!"

"No." Their mother set the bowl out of reach.
"Come wash up."

Luke looked disappointed, but he did what he
was told. "Yes, Mommy."

Their mom turned to Erin next. "And how was
your day?"

"Good." Erin didn't look up. She was sitting at
the counter reading. "We worked on pluses and
minuses." She peered over the tops of the pages. "I
have homework. I might need help."

Their mom walked around the counter to Erin.

25

She patted her hair. "Adding three-digit numbers. Very impressive."

"On my last one." Her answer was lightning fast.

"Two hundred and thirty-six plus two hundred and sixty. You sure you got it?" Her mom sounded extra proud, like she was sure Erin knew the answer.

"Yep." Erin wrote out the answer and set her pencil down. "Easy."

Ashley couldn't believe it. Erin was practically perfect. She never got a wrong answer and she always hung her backpack on the hook.

Mom looked proud. She gave Erin a kiss on the top of her head. "I think you'll do just fine." Her mom looked over Erin's shoulder. "*Charlotte's Web*. I love that book."

"Me, too!" Erin smiled up at their mother.

"That's my little reader." Their mom returned to the oven and removed another tray of cookies. This time the snickerdoodles must've been perfect because she set them on the counter. Then she looked again at Erin. "I'm proud of you, sweetheart."

Ashley crossed her arms and stared at her youngest sister. How did she do it? Erin had it all together in math and reading. And she wasn't even ten years old. Always so sweet and quiet.

Erin moved to the couch in the next room.

Ashley watched her. The truth was, she could never be like Erin. And she was okay with that. She could only be herself. Her very best self.

Their mom crossed the kitchen to Kari. "What about you, sweetheart? How was your day?" Mom untied her apron, folded it, and set it on the counter.

Kari's eyes got bright. "We're making dream collage boards." She did a little shrug. "I'm trying to figure out my dreams."

"That's important!" Their mom found a wet rag near the sink and started cleaning the counter. "So what have you come up with?"

Ashley listened. Maybe Kari had some new dreams since the bus.

But Kari just stared at her cookies and then back at their mom. "I guess I'm still thinking about that."

Was it ever going to be her turn? "Mom."

Ashley leaned back in her seat and crossed her arms. "Aren't you going to ask me?"

"Yes, dear." Her mother looked at her. "You were next."

"You mean I was *last*." Ashley took a bite of her cookie. "Because I didn't hang up my backpack, and because I'm always in trouble."

"No." Her mom's eyes were shiny, like maybe she was going to laugh. "You were last because you're sitting at that end of the counter, silly."

Ashley nodded. Maybe. That was a fair enough reason. Anyway, she raised her eyes at her mom. "So . . . aren't you going to ask me?"

"Ashley, please." This time an actual laugh came from her mom. "Give me a chance."

Fine. Ashley took another bite of her cookie and waited. Her mom walked around the counter and right up to her. She put her hand soft against Ashley's back. "And what about your day, my darling daughter?"

Darling sounded nice. Satisfaction came over her. "It was effervescent. Thank you for asking."

"Effer-what?" Luke gave her a confused look.

Their mom smiled at Luke. "It means . . . enthusiastic. Full of life." She turned back to Ashley. "Why was it effervescent?"

Ashley was proud of herself. Miss Wilson had challenged them to use *effervescent* in a sentence today, and now she had done it. She waited until everyone in the room was looking at her. "I have very big news." She sat taller on her stool and cleared her throat. "Yours truly is in charge of the class Valentine's Day party!"

"Ashley! That's wonderful." Her mom hugged her.

For the next ten minutes that's all everyone talked about. Even Erin put her book down and said she was excited for Ashley.

A smile filled Ashley's heart. Being last today wasn't the worst thing, after all. Her news was definitely the biggest of the afternoon.

When they were done talking Kari looked at her, and suddenly Ashley knew. This was the time. She mouthed the word, *Now*.

Kari seemed to understand exactly what she meant. Ashley watched her take a deep breath and turn back to their mom. "So . . . can Ashley and I please go skating . . . before homework?" Kari was expert at looking hopeful. Like a kid on Christmas morning. "Please? If we wash the pans first?"

Their mom was cleaning the counter again. She looked from Kari to Ashley. "Hmm . . . Homework should probably come first."

"Yes, Mom. But it'll be dark by then." Kari clasped her hands. "Please! If we don't stay out too long?"

Going off her sister's cue, Ashley brought her hands together, too. "Yes, please!"

Their mother seemed to think for a minute. "Okay." She smiled. "After the pans."

Ashley jumped right off the ground. "Woo-hoo! Thank you!" She raced Kari to the kitchen sink, where they did their fastest cleanup.

In no time the pans were put away and Ashley and Kari were decked in coats and scarves, gloves and snow pants. They flung their skates over their shoulders and headed out into the cold. The rink was five houses down, at the end of Keech Avenue in Allmendinger Park.

Ashley figured the next hour would be good for more than skating and dreaming.

It might even be effervescent.

The park rink was frozen solid, the ice more like thick cement. Ashley loved it that way, because at least she knew that she wouldn't fall through to the grass below, the way she had last spring when skating season was almost over.

Four other kids from the neighborhood were on the rink that afternoon. Ashley and Kari waved hello to them, then they laced up their skates and headed out onto the ice. They held hands the way they always did when they skated.

They talked about Lydia, and Kari's friend Brittany, and the Valentine's party in Ashley's class. "The first rule is everyone gets a valentine card." Ashley shook her head. "Sometimes Eric Powers forgets to give me one. I think on purpose."

"Eric Powers. He's that cute boy, right?" Kari whispered the words, like the kids across the rink might hear her.

31

"Definitely not." Ashley made a face. "He's the meanest boy in our class."

"Mean . . . but cute." Kari released Ashley's hand "Watch this!" She did a spin. For a minute she looked like a professional ice skater. She even lifted her leg in the air.

"Wow!" Ashley clapped her gloves together. She was never the most coordinated kid, but it didn't stop her from trying. "My turn." She picked up speed.

"Ashley!" From behind her, Kari sounded a little scared. "Are you sure?"

"Yes!" Ashley focused like an Olympic champion. "Look at this!" She felt her feet leave the ice, and suddenly she was in the air. Yes! She was doing it! This could be one more dream on her list. She felt graceful, like a beautiful ice skater.

Just like Kari.

Ashley was about to perform the most perfect landing when—*Whack!* She flopped onto the ice, sliding across the cold surface on her stomach.

Kari skated over to her in a hurry. She sounded scared to death. "Are you okay?"

Laughter made it easier for Ashley to catch her wind. Which was good, because laughter was something she was good at. "I'm fine." She sat up and pulled her knees to her chest.

Now Kari started laughing, too. She helped Ashley to her feet, but after a few more laps, they were still giggling about the fall.

"I think it might be time to go home." Ashley grinned at Kari. "A warm fire sounds perfect right about now."

They took off their skates and slipped back into their boots. And then they saw Sarah Grace coming toward them. She was walking her big furry brown dog, Roscoe.

"Hey, Kari. Hi, Ash." Sarah Grace stopped at the bench they were sitting on. Her dog sat down, panting. Like he was thirsty.

"Hey, SG." Kari pulled on her other boot and looked straight at her friend. "So . . . we saw the moving truck." Kari put her elbows on her knees and tilted her head. "I can't believe you're leaving."

Sarah Grace looked down at the ground. "Yeah. It all happened kind of fast. Because of my mom's job. We have to be in California right after Valentine's Day."

Ashley couldn't believe the news. "That's in ten days!" She zipped up her coat. "That's no actual warning."

"Even worse." SG put her hands in her pockets. "We leave Ann Arbor on Sunday." She frowned. The news was hard for her, Ashley could tell.

"We have to get back home." Kari stood and walked toward SG. "But we should hang out before you go."

"That'd be fun!" Sarah Grace smiled, still sad and defeated.

Kari hugged SG and then patted the dog's head. "Bye bye, Roscoe."

On the way home, Ashley and Kari passed the Johnson house again. They were both quiet, thinking about their chat with Sarah Grace. Ashley took a deep breath. "I feel sorry for the Johnsons. Moving must be hard."

"The worst." Kari shivered. They walked a few more steps and then Kari squeezed her hand. "Race you back!"

Kari got a head start, but Ashley caught up. And a few minutes later the girls were running up the sidewalk to home. Where, inside, Ashley knew the greatest mother in the world was making dinner, and the best dad ever would be home any minute. It was her whole world under one roof. They were the Baxter family, and they were her family.

The best family ever.

3

Valentine's Day Disaster

KARI

K ari wasn't sure how long her rope was, but she was definitely at the end of it. She didn't really know what that meant, but it sounded good. And she had heard her parents say it.

Her dad would come in after waiting in the car for too long and say, "Elizabeth, please hurry. I am at the end of my rope."

Kari heard that a lot.

Or when her mother would burn something in the kitchen she would say, "I am at the end of my rope here!"

Kari felt like she was almost out of rope because it was Valentine's Day and she couldn't decide what to wear. Yes, after days of listening to Ashley

36

talk about her party, and hours of giving her helpful tips, February 14 had finally arrived.

Ashley's party was going to be a hit. Their mom had taken her to buy streamers and banners and balloons. And the whole family had helped cut out paper hearts. Which turned out better than Ashley's first idea of snowflakes. All the pieces of a great party were in place.

Last night, all the Baxter kids had worked on their valentine cards. A few of them had the box kind from the store. But Kari made her own from card stock—pink for the girls and dark blue for the boys.

Now if only she could decide what to wear.

The bus was leaving in forty minutes and her bed was covered in outfits. She let out a deep breath and grabbed her old journal and a pen from the desk. Sometimes a girl just had to put her thoughts on paper. She flipped to the first clean page and dropped to her bed.

Today is already a disaster and it's not even eight in the morning! It's Valentine's Day and I don't know what to wear. Plus

Jason Jennings has been talking to me
way too much all week and I don't want
anything from him today. If he gives me a
giant box of candy in front of everyone like
he did last year, I'll be so embarrassed.
Cards from everyone. That would be better.
I just want to enjoy the day.
I think Valentine's Day is the worst day
of the year.

"Kari! Breakfast!" Her mom's voice from some-where downstairs broke the moment. "The bus leaves soon. Please hurry!"

Panic ran through Kari's veins. "Coming!" She returned to her journal:

More later. Gotta go!—Kari

Kari slipped the little book in her backpack and faced the mess around her. Pants, skirts, dresses, shirts, sweaters. It was like a tornado had come through and destroyed her room. Good thing Ashley was already dressed and downstairs.

"Okay, Kari. Just pick something . . . anything." She blew a piece of hair out of her face and put her hands on her hips. She wanted to wear a dress, but she didn't want to freeze. And she definitely didn't want Jason Jennings thinking she wore a dress for him. Of all things. But if she wore jeans, then *which* jeans. She rummaged through the pile of clothes, desperate.

Ashley walked into the room and completely ignored the disaster of it all. Which was one of the things Kari loved about Ashley, even if she didn't understand it. A messy room never bothered Ashley like it bothered Kari. Ashley walked to her bed and threw her backpack over her shoulder. Her hair was pulled into a high ponytail.

"Mom said you need to come down and eat or else." Ashley turned and looked at Kari. "You're still in pajamas?" Ashley's laugh sounded friendly. "You can't wear that."

"I'm not." Kari looked down. She wore a Johnson Elementary School T-shirt and flannel bottoms. "I can't decide what looks best."

"You look good in everything." Ashley flashed

her sister a nervous look as she grabbed her back-pack. "All I know is, you better hurry. The bus isn't going to wait." She headed out the bedroom door.

Kari rolled her eyes and flopped onto the pile of clothes on her bed. She yelled into her pillow, "This is the worst day. I'm ruined!" It felt good to get it out, especially since no one was listening.

But just then a knock sounded at the door. Kari rolled over to see her mom standing there. "Hi." She was leaning against the doorframe, her arms crossed. There wasn't even a hint of anger in her smiling face. "Happy Valentine's Day."

"Happy Valentine's Day." Kari tried to smile, too, but she felt embarrassed. "You heard me?"

"I did." Her mom came closer and sat on the edge of the bed. She took Kari's hand in hers. "Ashley said you were stressed?"

Kari couldn't hide the truth. "A little."

"You want to talk about it?" Her mom was in no hurry. Even if the bus was coming soon.

"Look at this." Kari motioned to the clothes piled up around her. "I don't know what to wear."

"Kari, honey . . ." Her mother sounded extra-kind. "It's not the clothes that matter, but the person in them."

Kari knew this was true, but it didn't help. She stood, exasperated. "Mom." The word came out like a cry for help. "I want to look good. This is a big day!" She shot another look at the clothes covering her bed. "Nothing's right."

"Maybe I can help." Calm and gentle, that was her mom as she joined in with the search. "Are you trying to look good for the party?"

Kari caught her mom looking at her, and she could feel herself turning red. "Yes. But not for Jason Jennings." She focused on the floor and a stack of jeans. "I told you about him, right?"

"You did." Her mom held up a top.

Kari shook her head. "Jason keeps trying to talk to me and everyone says he's going to give me a special valentine today, which is exactly what I don't want to happen." She threw her hands in the air very dramatic and flopped on the bed again. "But if it does happen and if everyone is looking at me, then I should at least have the right outfit. Not something that makes me look ten." She looked straight at her mom. "Does that make sense?"

"Of course." Her mother nodded. "We're going for ten, is that it?"

"Yes." Kari stood again. It was hopeless.

Just then her mom held up a pretty white sweater and a pair of dark jeans. "How about this?" Her mom looked at the clothes and back at Kari. "I'd say they're perfect."

"Wait." Kari studied them. "Actually . . . yes." She took the items from her mother. How had she missed these? "They *are* perfect."

"Now you'll be the best dressed girl in fifth grade."

Happiness came over Kari like sunshine on a rainy morning. Now the whole day was better. "Thank you." She took the clothes in her arms. "For everything."

Her mom stood and ran her fingers through Kari's hair. "You're a rare and beautiful girl, Kari. The clothes don't make that any more or less true." She smiled again. "Now get dressed. The bus won't wait." Her mom left the room and shut the door.

Kari dressed and hurried downstairs. She

grabbed a muffin and walked to the bus with her siblings. They made it just in time. Once they were seated, everyone was talking. Even the air felt like it was full of excitement.

A wonderful, buzzy sort of Valentine's Day thrill.

Kari clutched her bag of handmade cards.

Next to her on the seat, Ashley looked over and nudged her. "You okay?"

"I guess." Kari gave Ashley a weak smile. "I just don't want Jason to do anything weird. You know boys . . ."

"Yes, I do." Ashley nodded. "Most of them are great. But every now and then . . ."

Kari laughed and looked out the window. Sure, she thought Jason was funny. And okay, he was the fastest guy in her class. But she didn't want a boy liking her in the fifth grade. Too young! Plus three of the girls in their class already teased her about Jason. Apparently Jason was going around saying he thought Kari was pretty.

It was all too much. Kari just wanted to enjoy Valentine's Day with her friends.

"Kari?" Ashley tapped her shoulder.

She turned to her sister. "Yes?"

"I think that's a perfect outfit! It's gonna be a good day!"

"Thanks." Kari laughed and sighed at the same time. "You have your supplies for the party?"

"Right here." Ashley held up two bags. "Lydia is helping me set up at lunch. I can't wait!"

The rest of the bus ride was full of laughs and hopes for Valentine's Day. After the earlier talk with her mom and now with Ashley, Kari arrived at school feeling better than she had since she woke up. In fact, every student at Johnson Elementary seemed to be in a good mood. Nothing could ruin this day now.

Not even Jason Jennings.

Finally, after lunch, Mrs. Pike announced it was time to give out valentines. Kari joined the others, finding their bags of valentine cards and passing them out. Each student's desk had a paper basket on top to hold whatever they were given.

"I made mine myself." Brittany held up her cards

with hand-drawn hearts, butterflies, and words that read, *You're extra nice. Happy Valentine's Day!*

"Looks good!" Kari gave her friend a thumbs-up. "I made mine, too."

Jessica Howland sneered at both of them. Jessica always seemed sort of mean. She chuckled at Kari and Brittany. "My dad would never let me make valentine cards. He bought me the most expensive ones at the store." She held up a bag bursting with oversize chocolate bars. "Also, everyone gets candy." She looked Kari and Brittany up and down. "I bet you two didn't bring candy."

"Jessica, really?" Kari stared at the girl. "That's not nice."

The girl rolled her eyes. "I'm just saying . . ." She walked away, her voice trailing behind her, probably looking for the next classmate to tell. Kari was not impressed.

"Sorry, Brittany. She's so rude." Kari put her hand on Brittany's shoulder.

"It's fine." Brittany took a slow breath and stared at Jessica across the room. "Something must be wrong with that girl. That's what my mom always tells me about mean kids."

Kari smiled. "Mine, too. She says hurt people hurt people."

"Exactly." Brittany nodded. "You have to feel sorry for her."

The girls joined the rest of the class and passed out their cards. The excitement in the room made it impossible to worry too much about Jessica's mean words. Kari could hardly wait to open her valentines.

When they returned to their seats, Kari found a card sitting on her desk, a few inches away from her basket. Hand-drawn flowers and hearts decorated the envelope. *Please, God, not from Jason.*

Kari looked around as she opened it. Sure enough, it read: *Happy Valentine's Day to a Special Girl. Jason.*

A faint feeling came over Kari. This could not be happening. She had ignored Jason all week so this wouldn't happen. But still he hadn't gotten the message.

All the sudden she noticed Jason. He was standing a few feet away and he was holding a teddy bear. "Happy Valentine's Day, Kari." He handed her the stuffed animal. From the back of the class Kari heard a few students giggling.

She looked that way. Jessica was whispering to the girls around her.

Kari cleared her throat as she took the bear. She needed Jason to understand. She could almost hear her mom telling her that. Be yourself. That's what her mother would say. Kari found her smile. "Thank you, Jason. I only want to be friends. Just so you know."

He smiled. "I do. It's okay." He held a pen and now he took the card from her desk. He crossed out something and wrote some new words. When he handed it to her this time it read, *Will you be my friend?*

Everyone was watching. Kari could feel that. But Jason only smiled and gave her an easy shrug. "You can give the bear to your little brother if you want."

Suddenly Kari didn't care what the other kids said or whether Jessica Howland was making fun of her. Jason was only being nice. She took the bear and nodded. "I'll do that." She grinned at Jason. "Friends. Definitely."

"Great." Jason looked around. "Sorry. For the big scene. I told everyone I just wanted to be your friend." He gave her one last smile. "See you around."

"Sure." Relief filled Kari's heart. "See you."

Jason returned to his seat. Eventually Mrs. Pike took the front of the room and the moment was behind them. Kari couldn't have been happier.

Brittany leaned over. "You okay?"

"I am." Kari smiled. "Everyone needs friends."

"Yes." Brittany was on Kari's side for sure. "Exactly."

Kari promised herself she'd write about this in her journal later. She had been worried about nothing. Jason just wanted to be her friend.

Nothing more.

Which meant maybe she would even keep the teddy bear.

You could never have too many friends.

4

The Perfect Party

ASHLEY

Ashley couldn't believe the party was finally here. She and Lydia—with Miss Wilson's help—stretched crepe paper in rows across the top of the classroom, and they taped pink and red and white balloons in every corner.

"It has to be perfect." Ashley tied a string around a group of balloons near the doorway.

"It is!" Miss Wilson laughed. "You girls went way beyond what I expected."

Over the last few nights, Ashley and Lydia had decorated paper bags for their classmates. So when Ashley finished with the balloons, she set one bag on each desk. Then Lydia sprinkled confetti hearts around each one. So every desk was super decorated.

Next, Miss Wilson left to get plates and napkins from the cafeteria. While she was gone, Ashley and Lydia took the large hearts the Baxter family had cut out and taped them to the walls and the blackboard.

Finally they hung pink and white streamers from the top of the doorframe. So every boy and girl would walk through them after lunch. And last of all, the girls hung a Valentine's Day banner with the name of every student in their class. Ashley and Lydia stepped back and examined their work.

"You did it, Ashley." Lydia pushed her glasses up higher on her face. Then she looked around the room, clearly happy.

Ashley turned to her friend. "*We* did it." She gave Lydia a high five. Ashley surveyed the place. It was a wonderland of Valentine's Day perfection.

Miss Wilson came in through the pink and white streamers and gasped. "Girls, this is stunning! How exciting." She hurried the plates and napkins to her desk. "I have a little gift for you two." She pulled out a little box.

"What is it?" Ashley jumped in place a few times. Surprises were the best.

"Hold on." Miss Wilson laughed. She opened the box and pulled out two little heart pins. "These are for you girls. The best party makers in fourth grade." She helped the girls pin the hearts to their sleeves.

"They're beautiful, Miss Wilson." Ashley looked from their teacher to Lydia. "It's official. We really are extraordinaire!"

The bell rang and Miss Wilson checked her watch. "Do you need anything else?"

Just as their teacher finished talking, a group of boys came into the classroom, Eric Powers in the lead. Ashley winced a little. As far as she was concerned that meant just one thing.

Trouble.

"Touchdown!" Eric yelled before he even came into the room. Then he tore through the doorway, ripping down most of the pink and white streamers. The boys who followed brought down what remained.

Miss Wilson rushed to the pile of fallen streamers. She looked crushed. "Boys! Look what you've done. I'll talk with you both in a minute." She began to pick up the streamers lying in a mess on the floor.

It all happened so fast that Ashley didn't have time to be calm and breathe like normal. She picked up a handful of streamers and walked it to Eric. "How could you?"

"We didn't know." Eric threw his hands up like he was innocent.

But Ashley wasn't buying it. "You didn't know? Really? Well you want to know something now, Eric?" She threw the wad of streamers at his feet. "You just ruined Valentine's Day."

How could Eric do this? Ashley marched back over to Lydia, who was standing still. Like she was too shocked to move. Ashley put her hands on her hips. "We worked so hard."

"Yeah." Lydia sounded like she might cry. "Everything is ruined."

Ashley took a deep breath. She was mad, but she didn't want the day to be ruined. No matter what she had just told Eric. She looked at the boys, who were now getting a lecture from Miss Wilson.

I hope they get in big trouble, Ashley thought. *They deserve it.*

Eric came over, followed by the other boys. He looked right in her eyes. He was trying to be serious, but she could still see his smile. He wasn't good at hiding it.

"I'm sorry I ruined your decorations, Baxter." He swayed back and forth. "Now I gotta stay after school every day next week and organize Miss Wilson's bookshelves."

Ashley almost smiled at the news. Still, Eric didn't seem very sorry.

"It's *Ashley*." She crossed her arms. "And I don't believe you." She turned her head away. He didn't deserve her attention.

"Hey." Eric took a step toward her. "I'm sorry. Really." He tried to look right at her. "I wasn't careful. Truce?" He held out his hand.

Ashley stared at him. She was still really mad. But it was important to forgive people. Even enemies named Eric.

"Fine. I forgive you." She uncrossed her arms. She shook his hand and then walked to the damage zone. Lydia was already there, helping Miss Wilson.

"Boys." Their teacher stood up. "Come help. All of you."

The boys did as they were told. They gathered the streamers and in a few minutes they had them taped back where they belonged.

Lydia leaned close to Ashley and whispered. "I can't believe you forgave him."

"It was the right thing to do." Ashley picked up the ripped banner, which had also fallen when the boys rushed in. "Come on. Help me get this taped up again."

"Here." Miss Wilson brought some wider tape, and together the three of them tried to rehang the banner. But it didn't look the same.

"I'm sorry, Ashley." Miss Wilson put her arm around Ashley's shoulders. "The room still looks amazing."

Lydia nodded as she looked around. "It really does."

They were right. Ashley had to agree. The other kids wouldn't notice the banner and streamers being slightly off. It was still going to be the best possible Valentine's party. And a class could have perfect fun without perfect decorations. Because no one and nothing except God was perfectly perfect.

Ashley's dad had taught her that.

She smiled and took a deep breath. She felt better already.

Finally the other students came back from lunch. Every one of them walked through the streamers, slow and careful. Miss Wilson stood at the door and made sure they all got to their seats without taking any of the other decorations down.

Ashley watched her classmates, then she looked at Lydia. "They like it."

Lydia was studying the other boys and girls, too. "They love it."

Sure, Ashley's decorations didn't go as planned, but the party was still a success. And her game Pin the Arrow on Cupid was a hit. Eric Powers was way far off from the target. Ashley and Lydia couldn't help feeling good about that after what had happened earlier.

"At least now I know why you couldn't walk through the door without tearing down the streamers." Ashley said the quiet words so only Eric could hear them. "You're a little clumsy."

"You got me there, Baxter." He grinned at her. "I did say I was sorry, you know."

"I know." She lifted her chin. "But maybe you shouldn't have done it in the first place. Unless you really are clumsy."

"I'm not clumsy." Eric rolled his eyes. "I'll pay better attention next time."

At the end of the day, Ashley believed with all her heart that it was the best Valentine's Day party. Better than she and Lydia had dreamed. Ashley knew it had a bit to do with her attitude.

She thought of something else her dad always said. Sometimes you just need to be like a duck and let the water roll off your back. And her dad was usually right.

As she sorted through her valentine cards, she noticed that she didn't get a special one, like Kari was worried about.

Ashley was so glad.

Better to have lots of friends in her class. It would be so embarrassing if someone like Eric

Powers ever actually liked her and gave her some special valentine. No thank you.

Also the day was great because of the heart pin from Miss Wilson.

Their teacher thanked them again as the bell rang that afternoon.

"It was a beautiful party." Miss Wilson looked at the two of them. "You and Lydia were just the right people for the job."

Ashley lifted her hand to give Miss Wilson a high five, then she changed her mind. Maybe not for a teacher. Instead she gave Miss Wilson the biggest smile she had. Outside she met her siblings by the bus. Everyone had a bag full of cards and candy. They climbed on and took their seats. This time the students were quiet, the energy from the morning all used up.

Luke tapped Ashley on the shoulder. "Did you get a lot of valentimes?" His mouth was full of chocolate.

"Valen*tines* . . . With an *n* . . ." Ashley drew the letter *n* in the air with her finger. "And yes, I got a few." She held up her bag of goodies. "Looks like you got candy!"

"We did! We had the bestest party!" Luke took the bag and rummaged through it, grabbing a handful of chocolate. "Look at all this!"

"Don't eat it all at once!" Ashley laughed and then she turned to Kari. She was dying to hear how her sister's day had gone. "Well? What happened?"

"You first!" Kari bounced a little on the bus seat. "Tell me about your party. Did everyone love it?"

"They did." Ashley raised her fist into the air. "It was perfect!" Ashley felt her smile fall off. "Except the part where Eric Powers and his football buddies tore down half the decorations before the other kids got to the classroom."

"No!" Kari's eyes grew wide. "That's terrible."

"Yes." Ashley didn't have anything else to say, it was over and she wasn't going to be mad about it anymore. "Miss Wilson helped us fix it. So everything was okay." Ashley searched her sister's eyes. "Your turn."

"First . . ." Kari unzipped her backpack and pulled out a teddy bear. "I got this from Jason."

"Yikes! Just what you were afraid of." Ashley couldn't believe it. "What did he say?"

"He said . . . he just wants to be friends." She looked at the bear. "And that I could give the bear to Luke."

In the seat in front of them, Luke spun around. "You got me a bear."

Kari laughed. "I'm going to keep it, bud."

Ashley lowered her chin and raised her eyebrows. "You're *keeping* it?"

"That's what you do, right?" Kari looked at the bear again. "If a friend gives you something, you keep it."

Ashley was shocked. "Since when is Jason your friend?" Ashley couldn't believe what she was hearing. Jason was always digging holes at recess. He smelled like eggs.

"No, I don't like him." Kari shook her head. "He's nice. That's all." Kari looked at Ashley. "As a *friend*."

"So, then what's wrong?" Ashley felt like Kari wasn't telling the whole story. She was so quiet.

Kari thought for a bit. She did that a lot. Then she looked at Ashley. "Well . . . at lunch, he was talking to Jessica and Katy. So it felt like he didn't really mean it. Like he has lots of friends. Nothing special."

Ashley crossed her arms. How could a boy do that to her sister? Give her a big friend gift and then be friends with other girls at lunch? So rude. "Some boys ruin everything. Lydia said that earlier. I think it's true."

Kari giggled. "Sometimes. I guess."

As they got off the bus Ashley spotted their dad waiting by his car.

"Daddy!" Ashley ran and jumped into his arms. He picked her up and spun her around.

"My little princess!" Their father was tall and strong, full of energy and happiness. Like always.

He set Ashley down and then he picked up Kari and then Erin and twirled them the same way. Luke was last and their dad hugged him and gave him a high five. Then one at a time he handed Ashley and Kari and Erin each a long-stemmed red rose. "Happy Valentine's Day to my favorite girls." He swooped Erin into his arms. "I gave one to Brooke and to your mother earlier." He looked at Luke and pulled out a chocolate bar from his pocket. "And I couldn't forget about my little man. Happy Valentine's Day, Luke!"

Luke's eyes grew wide as he grabbed the bar. "More candy! Thanks, Dad!" He tore open the wrapper and started eating.

Erin studied his hospital work badge. "Did you help lots of people today, Daddy?"

"Yes." Their father nodded, confident. "God always gives me eyes to know how to help them."

Ashley smiled, proud. Her dad was the best doctor in the world, and really good at helping people.

"Guess what?" Ashley's dad's eyes danced from her to her siblings and back again. He was really excited. "I'm taking Erin and Luke to a movie. And Mommy has a surprise for you older girls at home."

Ashley was confused, a surprise? Better than going to the movies? She put her thumb and finger on her chin, like she was solving a mystery. "The movies sound fun, Daddy. Can't we go?"

Dad winked at her. "I think you'll like this

surprise." He helped Erin and Luke into the car. Then he kissed the girls on their cheeks and sent them on their way.

Ashley looked at Kari as the car drove off. "I guess we should see what Mom's doing." The girls walked down the road toward their house, the snow crunching under their feet.

Ashley thought about the surprise. "Maybe it's brownies."

"No." Kari kept her eyes straight ahead. "She makes those all the time."

"True." Ashley kept walking, waiting for other ideas to come. "A horse! That has to be it!"

Kari stopped and looked at her. She blinked a few times. "A horse? Where would it sleep?"

Ashley didn't hesitate. "The mudroom. Of course."

"I don't think so." Kari kept walking and Ashley stayed right with her. "You need a barn for a horse."

"Yeah but . . . I've been wanting a horse for a year. At least." Ashley paused. "I was going to name her Frenchie. Also I've been thinking. And I want our soccer team to be called the Mighty Dolphins."

"First, Ashley." Kari shook her head. "Mom did

not buy you a horse." A smile flashed on her face then. "And second . . . I love that name. Mighty Dolphins."

Even though she'd brought up the team name, Ashley couldn't think about soccer. Not when she was wondering about the surprise. She sighed. Maybe it wasn't a horse. So then what was it?

When they made it inside, the house smelled wonderful. Like vanilla cake. And pretty music played softly from somewhere. Ashley and Kari took their shoes off and Kari hung her backpack.

Ashley did the same. She wanted to be extra-careful not to upset her mom. Especially when she had a big surprise planned.

Just then, Brooke came through the door. She looked like she'd been crying.

"I thought you'd be home by now." Kari spoke first. "What's wrong?"

"Everything." Brooke hung her bag on the third hook and sniffed. "I guess in middle school, not everyone gives valentine cards." Her eyes filled up. "I didn't get a single valentine from any boys in my class. I'm the only one."

"What?" Ashley couldn't believe it. "Why?"

"They don't like me." Her voice was frustrated and sad. "Obviously."

Ashley didn't know what to say. How could that happen? At Kennedy Middle School everyone loved Brooke. Even the teachers. She was the perfect student. Just like Erin.

"I'm sorry." Kari reached for Brooke's hand. "That's rotten. It really is."

"It doesn't matter." Brooke sniffed again. "I hate Valentine's Day."

Ashley held out her bag of candy. "You can have some of mine."

Brooke let out a laugh that was more like a cry. "Thanks, Ash." She took a piece of chocolate. "Where is everyone?"

Just then, their mother came into the entryway. She didn't notice Brooke's expression right away. Instead she motioned to the three of them. "Follow me!" She looked like she was holding in a secret. "Happy Valentine's Day, girls."

Whatever the surprise was, they were about to find out.

5

Being Princesses

KARI

Kari's stomach had butterflies. She loved surprises, especially ones from their mother. Hers were always the best. And no, this wasn't going to be a horse. Kari was sure of that.

The three of them followed their mom into the front dining room.

Everywhere they looked the place was decorated with pink and white and red balloons, and streamers the same colors looped across the ceiling. The table had a white cloth, and over that, in perfect settings, sat what looked like brand-new china and silver.

The whole room was like something from a Valentine's Day fairy tale.

"This is amazing," Kari whispered.

"Wow!" Even Brooke smiled. Her sadness was clearly gone for the moment. "Mom, this is the prettiest thing ever."

"That settles it." Ashley nodded. "You and I have the same decorating skills."

A large bouquet of white roses sat at the center of the table. They were so pretty they almost didn't look real. But the smell filled the dining room. Kari was still trying to take it all in.

Soft jazzy music played from a CD player in the corner, and Kari immediately recognized the song. It was "You Are My Sunshine." "Hey! We sang that in school today!" Kari had never smiled so big.

Her mother took hold of Kari's hands and they started to dance, singing along to the music. "You are my sunshine, my only sunshine."

Ashley and Brooke held hands and danced, too. Though they didn't know all the words the way Kari did. When the song ended, Kari saw something else. Near the teacups and saucers were gift bags. One for each of them.

This just kept getting better, she thought.

Kari looked at Ashley and Brooke. Then the three of them turned to their mother. "A tea party?" Kari spoke first. "Is that what this is?"

"You'll see." Their mother smiled and headed for the kitchen. "Find your name and have a seat. I'll be right back."

Kari looked at her sisters, wide eyed, mouth open. They sprang into action, looking for their names. Kari found hers next to Ashley and her mom. Her name was written on a sealed letter near her pink and white gift bag.

"This is the best!" Brooke squealed. She brought her hands to her face. "And look at these cups!"

Kari picked up the teacup in front of her. It was pink and gold, with delicate flowers. She might as well have been a real princess. True royalty!

The girls took their seats, and minutes later, their mom came into the room with a tray of treats and a pot of tea.

"Teatime!" She placed the tray in the center of the table and took her chair.

For a few seconds, Kari looked at Brooke. She actually seemed happy now. Kari was glad.

Brooke took hold of their mom's hand. "So beautiful, Mom. Thanks." She smiled. "I needed this today."

For the first time Mom seemed to notice something was wrong. She moved Brooke's bangs from her eyes. "What happened, honey?"

"Middle school is hard." Brooke sank back against her chair.

Kari tried to help out. "No valentine cards from any of the boys." Kari gave Brooke a sympathetic look. "I'm definitely not looking forward to middle school."

"Me, either." Ashley tapped her teacup. "At least I have two years until I'm in sixth grade. That's practically forever."

"Well." Mom looked from Brooke to Kari and then Ashley. "This is good timing, then. You girls are princesses. You are priceless. One in a million. I want you to always remember that, every time Valentine's Day comes around." Her smile reached all the way to Kari's heart. Their mom continued, "What better way to celebrate a day of love than with a princess tea party? All of us together!" She took hold of the teapot. "Now, let's get started!"

The girls sat up straight, swapping smiles. Mom had shared beautiful moments with them all their lives. But nothing like this.

"In England, tea is proper. Just like princesses are. So, if you add sugar or cream, don't clink the sides of the cup with the spoon." She passed around the sugar dish and the creamer.

Kari watched her mother grab one sugar cube, so Kari did the same.

Their mother held up the tea and mini plate. "Hold the saucer in one hand while you drink with the other." She took a sip. "And never slurp." Putting on her best British accent, their mom lifted her chin, all proper-like. "It's not polite to slurp, don't you agree?"

The girls giggled. Each of them did her best to imitate their mother.

Kari held her pinkie finger out as she took the slightest sip. She also attempted a British accent. "The tea is marvelous, Mother." She loved the way it tasted. And she felt so grown up.

"Yes, dahhling." Ashley held her cup up toward

Kari and then Brooke. "Marvelous, Mother."

"Truc, truc." Even Brooke gave a try at an English accent. "You make the most lovely tea, dear *mum*."

Next Mom passed around the tray of treats. There were finger sandwiches, scones, shortbread cookies, and chocolates. All were homemade, all delicious, and all made with love. The way their mom always baked. Kari could picture her working all day to make this the perfect Valentine's Day tea party. She smiled.

Their mother sure knew how to make them feel loved.

Kari took a bite of the scone. Cranberry. Absolutely perfect.

Across the table Ashley took a sip of her tea and made a silly face.

"Not a fan?" Their mom gave Ashley a sympathetic look. "It took me a few years to acquire a taste for tea."

"No! It's good!" Ashley shook her head a little. "Really. Just . . . well, maybe a little strong."

"Mum." Brooke raised her teacup in their

mother's direction. "Please pass the sugar to my dear sister Ashley."

"Yes. A whole lot of sugar, if you please." Ashley's fake British accent was so thick it made them all laugh.

Mom passed the dish of sugar cubes, and without hesitating Ashley dropped four cubes into her tea. A light bit of laughter came from their mother. "Usually just one or two, Ashley. So you can taste the tea still."

Ashley looked embarrassed, but she smiled as she stirred the tea. "So, I'm a princess with a sweet tooth." She shrugged. "I'm always a little different."

"True." The comment made Mom laugh even harder. She covered her mouth with her napkin.

The girls snacked on the treats and sipped tea and then their mother looked at each of them. "So, how was Valentine's Day?" She asked the question softly. Like she cared a lot about their answers.

"Well . . ." Brooke set her cup down, cleared her throat and looked at Mom. "It's like Kari said. A lot of my friends got valentines. You know, telling them they were funny or cute." She paused and took a breath. "But not me. I didn't get one. I guess I just felt . . . not very special."

Ashley shook her head, clearly upset. "A bunch of boys almost ruined my party decorations. They ripped down streamers and destroyed my banner." She gave Brooke a look of sympathy. "I definitely get it about boys." Ashley took another sip of her tea and chomped down on a scone. "Who needs them?"

Kari had an idea. "Hey, Brooke. You can have the valentine that Jason gave me! It's a big teddy bear. He said he wanted to be my friend, but he spent all lunch talking to these other girls." She hesitated. "So you can have it if you want."

"Are you kidding?" Brooke frowned. "You got a Valentine's gift from a boy? You're only in fifth grade!" Brooke slumped in her chair. "It's okay. Thanks. You can keep your bear."

Did she say something wrong? Kari had the feeling she did.

Ashley leaned over. "Nice going. Now you hurt Brooke's feelings."

"Kari didn't hurt anyone's feelings." Their mother stepped in. With so many kids she always knew how to be a good peacemaker.

Kari slumped in her chair. "I was only trying to help."

Their mom exhaled. "Well . . . seems like we had an eventful Valentine's Day. And sounds like all your stories have something in common. Hurt feelings." Her voice was as gentle as a breeze. "Girls, listen. People will always hurt you. They'll let you down. They may be unkind or annoy you or frustrate you. Worst of all they might not appreciate you."

Kari thought about Jessica, and how she didn't think anyone's valentine cards were as good as hers. "You're right." Kari's voice was soft.

"Definitely." Brooke nodded.

"Some of the boys in my class are like that." Ashley folded her arms.

Mom sat back in her chair and took a slow breath. "That's why you have to be confident in who you are, in the girls God made you to be."

Kari liked how that sounded. The idea that no matter who was around her or who was annoying her, or not appreciating her, she could be confident in who she was.

"It's still difficult." Brooke seemed to be really listening to their mother. "How do you get to be that confident?"

"Well"—their mom took another sip of her tea—"you focus on being the best Brooke Baxter you can be. That means loving God and yourself and loving those around you. Being kind even when others aren't. And, at the end of the day, knowing that you did all you could to make this world a better place." She paused to let that sink in. "That's where you put your time and effort."

Kari had never thought of things like this before. Her mother's wisdom was exactly what she needed. She looked at Mom. "You mean like, we can't worry about other people? So we should just focus on what good we can do?"

"Exactly." Mom smiled. "Most of us could be busy full-time trying to be the best versions of ourselves." She looked at each of the girls. "Of course, you won't be perfect. No one ever is. But that's where faith comes in. Faith that God's not finished with us yet."

"I like that." Brooke looked like she had a lot on her mind. "Then you won't feel the sadness as much when people aren't nice to you."

"Now you're getting it." Their mom set her teacup down.

Kari had a question. "What if someone is fake? They act nice but they really aren't?"

Mom's eyes were soft. "Like what happened with Jason?"

Kari felt her cheeks get hot. "He acted like I was his favorite person. Then at lunch he didn't even talk to me. It wasn't nice."

"No, it wasn't." Mom took hold of Kari's hand again. "I'm sorry he hurt your feelings. But maybe he didn't see you there. We have to give people the benefit of the doubt."

"Like grace?" Kari understood what her mom meant. They'd talked about grace at church a few weeks ago. It meant to do something nice for someone else, even if they didn't deserve it. You give them a second chance.

And that is called grace.

"Exactly, Kari." Their mom poured each of them a bit more tea. "Here's what I want you to hold on to." She looked at each of them, one at a time. "The right kinds of friends will be careful with your heart. Because you girls are the most beautiful treasures. True princesses." She paused. "Remember that always."

Wow. Kari had never felt so magnificent in all her life.

"I feel more beautiful now." Brooke sat a little straighter. "Thanks, Mom. Today was perfect."

Ashley took another scone. "Even better than my Valentine's party." She raised her eyebrows at their mom. "And that's saying a lot cause my party was pretty amazing."

"We'll do this again soon." Mom held up her teacup. "More tea parties. Sound good?"

The girls all agreed. Kari could hardly wait for whatever they might talk about at the next one. Then their mom asked God out loud to protect the Baxter girls. Also that the girls would feel the love of Jesus today and every day. And that they would know how truly special they were.

After that, their mother let them open their gift bags.

While her sisters went through theirs, Kari opened the letter first. A beautiful flower covered the front and on the inside her mom had written a scripture. Proverbs 3:5–6. *Trust in the Lord with all your heart and lean not on your own understanding; in all your ways submit to Him and He will make your paths straight.*

Beneath that she had written:

Kari, You are brave, beautiful, intelligent and oh so wonderful. Trust God with everything. He will lead you to your future, to your dreams. I love you. Happy Valentine's Day! Love, Mom.

Kari looked up at her mom. "Thanks, Mom." She jumped up and hugged her mother's shoulders. "That's the sweetest note."

Her mother kissed her cheek. "You're welcome. I love you. Open your gift!"

While her sisters did the same thing, Kari pulled the tissue paper out of the bag and lifted out two gifts. A small book full of daily Bible verses and encouragement. And a brand-new pink journal. She ran her fingers over the leather cover and flipped through the crisp, lined pages. "These are perfect."

"They are!" Brooke and Ashley added their enthusiasm. Each of them had gotten the same book and a similar journal.

Kari finished going through the bag. Lip gloss, candy, fuzzy pink pens, and three beaded bracelets. She exchanged excited looks with her sisters, who'd each gotten various versions of the same thing.

As beautiful as it all was, Kari loved her new book best. She would read it tonight, before writing in her journal.

When they stood to clear the teacups, Kari hugged her mom. "What you said, it was the best advice ever."

Her mom patted her face. "I'm the most blessed mom to have girls like you."

They were cleaning up when Dad came home with Luke and Erin. The movie must've been great, because they were still laughing about it. That's when their mom pulled out two more gift bags from the kitchen cupboard. One for Erin and another for Luke.

As her youngest siblings opened their bags, Kari smiled to herself. She would never forget tonight. They had the sweetest, most thoughtful, most understanding mother in all the world. And because of her, they had something else.

The best Valentine's Day ever.

Once they were in bed that night, Kari read her new book by flashlight. Ashley did the same thing. So far Kari had read three days' worth of encouragement. The book was even better than she had hoped.

"Listen to this." Ashley flipped her covers off and sat straight up in bed. She shone the light at Kari.

"Not in my eyes!" Kari squinted. "And don't yell. You'll wake up Erin and Luke."

"Sorry." Ashley did a quiet nervous-sounding laugh. She lowered her voice. "You gotta hear this. It's like it was written just for me."

"Mine's that way, too." Kari sat up. "What does yours say?"

Ashley used her flashlight to see the words. "It

says we are the clay and God is the potter!" Again she seemed to work to keep her voice quieter. "That means God is an artist! Just like me!"

Enthusiasm was something Kari loved about her younger sister. "Or maybe you're an artist like He is." She shifted so she could see Ashley better.

"So we really are princesses!" Ashley smiled and pulled her knees to her chest, excited.

Kari smiled at her sister. "Royalty, dahhhling!"

They giggled and then Ashley shushed Kari. "Do you hear that? It's music." Ashley jumped out of bed and tiptoed to the door. "Come on." She looked back.

"Okay." Kari could barely hear the sound, but Ashley was right. Someone was playing a song. She followed Ashley into the hallway.

Brooke's door opened at the same time and she poked her head out. Her eyes were barely half open. "What's happening?"

"Shhh." Ashley put her finger to her mouth. "Come with us. We're gonna find out!"

The three girls snuck down the stairs just far enough so they could see the kitchen. Their parents were dressed up, like they were going on a date. Kari watched as her dad took a tray of chocolate-covered strawberries from the fridge and turned the music up.

"John." Their mom grinned. "The kids are sleeping!"

"They're fine." He put his hands on her waist and pulled her close. Then he kissed her lips. "Happy Valentine's Day, Elizabeth Baxter."

Their mother giggled. "Happy Valentine's Day, John Baxter. You're my favorite forever."

Her favorite forever? Kari looked at her sisters. All of them had sparkly eyes. This was the best, seeing their parents dance and love each other like this.

Dad held Mom's hand out and the two of them began to dance. They twirled around the kitchen to the music, and their father spun her under his arm and pulled her back in.

They were good at it.

"Remember"—their dad spoke soft, straight into their mother's eyes—"that long-ago dance?"

"When we first met?" Their mom's cheeks were a deeper pink now. "How could I ever forget?"

Kari tried to figure out the look on her dad's face. It was like he was seeing their mom for the first time. The two of them clearly had a beautiful love. Something all the Baxter kids had seen.

But they'd never seen it quite like this.

As she sat there with her sisters at the top of the stairs, Kari couldn't take her eyes off her parents. Because love like this was the most beautiful thing Kari had ever seen. And one day, when she was older, she wanted the kind of love her parents shared.

Maybe tomorrow she would ask her parents to dance in the kitchen again. So she could take a picture of them. Kari smiled. She knew just where she would put it.

Right in the middle of her dream collage board.

6

Saturday Morning

ASHLEY

Ashley climbed out of her covers and ran to her bedroom window. Her heart sank to her ankles. More snow. It was the first Saturday in March and still spring wasn't here.

She walked back to her bed very soft on her feet, so she wouldn't wake Kari.

Miss Wilson had said spring would be here soon because of March coming up. But it was March and the snow wasn't melting. Not even a little.

"What are you doing?" Kari whispered. She turned on her side and gave Ashley a funny look. "We're supposed to sleep in on Saturdays."

"I'm not tired." Ashley let her legs dangle over the edge of her bed. "I want to take a bike ride."

"Now? In the snow?" Kari giggled. "You're the funniest person I know."

"Not now." Ashley stood and went to the window again. She sat on the sill and looked at her sister. "I mean, yes now. But not now because it's too snowy. And honestly I'm just a little tired of the snow."

Kari sat up. "What time is it?"

"Seven-thirty." Ashley glanced over her shoulder at the bedside clock, and then back at Kari. "I guess I thought the snow would melt. Because it's March." She paced a few steps away from the window and back again. "Honestly. Snow should have a limit."

"I thought you loved snow." Kari shook her head like she was puzzled. "Remember? Twirling like a snowflake? Wishing your teacher would hold class outside?"

Ashley stared out the window. Her shoulders sank some. "That's different." She walked with slow steps back to her bed and sat on the edge again. "I love fresh snow." She pointed outside. "That stuff is old and crusty. Dirty and icy. The worst snow of all."

Pans rattled downstairs in the kitchen. Ashley jumped up. "That's Mom! I'll go help her make breakfast."

"You do that." Kari slid back under the covers. "See you in an hour."

"Maybe the snow will be melted by then." Ashley laughed as she ran out of the room.

"You should have your own TV show," Kari called after her.

A TV show. Ashley tossed the idea around in her head while she ran down the stairs. Sure. She could add that to the list. She could do as many things as she wanted.

When she reached the kitchen she found Brooke instead of their mother. "Oh." Ashley slumped a bit. "It's you."

Brooke looked at her for a few seconds before her smile arrived. "Good morning to you, too."

Ashley laughed. "Sorry." She walked to Brooke and gave her a side hug. "Good morning."

Brooke was stirring something. Eggs, maybe.

"What are you making?" Ashley put her elbows on the counter and rested her chin in her hands.

85

Brooke looked determined. "An omelet. But we're out of cheese."

"Mom said she's making pancakes." Ashley looked toward the stairs. "Whenever she wakes up."

"Eggs are healthier." Brooke stirred while she looked at Ashley. "I'm going to be a food scientist one day. I'll make a whole book of the best recipes so everyone can be healthy. A scientist makes life better for people."

Ashley couldn't help but ask herself, *Who wakes up on a Saturday dreaming of being a scientist?* Pancakes were as far as Ashley's goals for the day went. That and maybe having her own TV show. "I will say, Brooke, pancakes taste better." Ashley leaned back. "But you'll definitely be a good scientist. That's for sure."

After a few minutes, Ashley couldn't take any more waiting. Where was her mother, and where were her pancakes? She walked back upstairs and heard noises from her youngest siblings' room. Louder and louder. *Good.* Ashley smiled. The more noise they made, the greater the chance their mother would wake up.

Luke and Erin's bedroom door was open. Theirs was the biggest room, but they slept in a bunk bed. That's because it was also the playroom.

"What's happening in here?" Ashley stepped into the room.

Luke beamed at her, his arms full of toys. "We're playing who-can-build-the-highest-tower-from-all-the-toys-in-the-room." His words ran together. "I'm going to win!"

"I never heard of that game." Ashley laughed. She loved Luke's happy spirit.

"Yes. Whoever makes the tallest tower before it falls is the winner." Erin giggled. "Luke keeps beating me."

No wonder the game was so loud. They weren't even being careful. Luke threw a dump truck on a toy piano, and a doll on top of that. Whatever they could grab. Every few seconds someone's tower would fall to the floor.

At that instant both Erin's and Luke's towers fell. "This is the funnest time!" Luke jumped in place before starting another tower.

Something caught Ashley's eye and she looked

through the bedroom door just as their mother walked in. Her worried look lightened when she saw toys all over the floor. "What in the world . . ." She laughed. "I thought the house was falling apart."

"It's the best game, Mom." Luke started his description all over again.

Their mom really seemed interested, which was one of Ashley's favorite things about her. Because actually, stacking toys on top of each other wasn't fascinating.

Pretty soon Dad joined them and he got to hear about Luke's game, too. Then he and Mom told them the best news. They were going to Hilton Head, South Carolina, for spring break, which was in just a few weeks. Dad had it all planned. He and Mom had rented a house right on the beach! So they could walk outside and play in the sand and enjoy sunny days and splash around in the waves.

Depending on how warm it was.

"Yes! Sun. Bye- bye, snow!" Ashley did a victory dance. "Do you think we'll see any sea animals?"

"Possibly!" Her dad's face lit up. "Fish for sure! Probably some crabs and starfish."

"I want to see a dolphin!" Erin jumped up and down, like she was already there on the shore.

"Maybe we could snorkel." Luke sounded hopeful.

"That would be the best." Ashley watched her dad pretend to snorkel with Luke, and they all laughed. Excitement for the trip was building.

Brooke walked up. "This is going to be the best spring break ever." She cheered.

Ashley knew she was right. Because the beach meant no snow. She looked out the window and closed her eyes. A few weeks was at least twenty days. Ashley could hardly wait to count down the exact number till spring break. The most epic, snowless, perfect, warm spring break ever!

They continued celebrating, and a little while later, everyone wound up in the kitchen, where Ashley *finally* helped Mom make pancakes. The part she thought would be the highlight of the morning. And it was fun. Ashley loved cooking with her mom.

But the best part of that morning was the time with her family. Because snowy Saturdays might not be good for bike rides. But they were great for something even better.

Being with family.

7

A Family Meeting

KARI

Spring break was finally here! They were leaving for South Carolina in the morning and Kari couldn't wait.

Her parents had called a family meeting for six o'clock that night. Probably to go over details of the trip. The meeting was in fifteen minutes and Kari still had a lot to do. She pulled out her journal and looked at what was left on her packing list.

1. Swimsuit
2. Shorts
3. Shirts
4. Pajamas
5. Sweatshirt in case it's cold

6. ~~Flip-flops~~
7. Goggles

Kari bit down on the end of her pen. *Goggles.* They were around here somewhere. She looked at Ashley, stretched out on her bed drawing in her new journal.

"You're supposed to write in it." Kari walked closer to her sister. "Not draw pictures."

"I like drawing better." Ashley smiled at her.

Kari squinted her eyes. "Have you packed?"

"Nope." Ashley smiled again.

"You're running out of time." Kari couldn't believe how Ashley always waited until the last minute. "Family meeting, remember?" Kari breathed out harder than before. Her sister was never going to get it all done.

"I'll pack later." Ashley kept moving her pencil across the page. "I'm drawing our house. Because it's the best house in the world." She looked up. "What do you think this family meeting is about?"

Kari ignored her last question. "Right now? Right now you have to draw our house?"

"It felt that way." Ashley giggled. "Sometimes my brain just works like that."

A laugh slipped out because Ashley was the funniest sister in the family. She had so much spirit. "About the meeting . . . it's probably about the trip. All the details." Kari dropped to the floor and looked under her bed. "Where are my goggles? I can't find them."

"Not sure." Ashley was back at her artwork. "Try Brooke's closet." She glanced up again. "So you don't think it's bad news? The meeting?" Fear flashed in her eyes. "I'm a little worried about that."

"It's nothing." Kari headed for the door. "What bad news could there be? We're leaving for South Carolina in the morning."

"True." Ashley looked back at her drawing. "Thanks."

"Sure." Kari walked down the hall and poked her head into her oldest sister's room. "Hey, Brooke? Have you seen my goggles?"

"Not lately." Her oldest sister was packing clothes into her duffel bag. "There's a box of summer stuff in my closet."

Kari stared at her sister. Brooke was neat, obedient, always making friends, a hard worker, and never ran late. Kari wanted to be just like her. She opened the closet door. Sure enough. Her goggles were on top of the box. "Yes!" She held them up. "I needed these."

Brooke faced her. "So . . . this family meeting. What do you think Mom and Dad want to tell us?"

"Stuff about the trip, I guess." Kari grinned. "And now I'm officially ready for it."

"What about Ashley?" Brooke sat on the edge of her bed.

"She's drawing."

"Of course." Brooke laughed. "Hours before a trip." She looked in the mirror opposite her bed and smoothed her hair. "What about Erin and Luke?"

"Probably building that toy tower again." Kari raised one eyebrow. "Let's go find out." They hurried out of Brooke's room and headed to Luke and Erin's. Brooke opened the door and stopped. Their two youngest siblings were on their beds reading. Two suitcases stood packed nearby.

"Well, look at you two!" Brooke leaned against the doorframe, her arms crossed.

"Amazing." Kari stood just behind her, checking the room. "You two are fast!"

"Yep." Luke gave them a thumbs-up. "All ready."

"Mom helped." Erin was reading *Stuart Little*. She had finished *Charlotte's Web* a long time ago. A book a week, that's how much Erin liked to read.

"Okay." Brooke stepped back. "See you at the family meeting."

Kari and Brooke both hurried down the hallway to their rooms. Kari found Ashley was putting shorts in her bag. It was about time.

"Someone at school said Hilton Head has tons of kids our age." Ashley looked up at Kari. "Do you think that's true?"

Kari dropped to the comfy chair in the corner of their room. "I don't know. Maybe." She thought for a few seconds. "It doesn't matter. Spring break is for family."

Ashley gathered a few shirts from their dresser. "Yeah. I know." She zipped her bag shut, and flopped down on her bed. "But new friends can be fun."

"Family meeting!" Their mom's voice echoed through the upstairs hallway. She didn't sound worried. Kari felt herself relax. She had been right all along. The meeting was about the trip.

It had to be.

Still. Now that it was here, Kari wasn't sure. Brooke and Ashley had been a little worried about it. So maybe she should've been worried, too.

Ashley got off the bed first. Kari followed her into the hallway.

"Do you think this is going to be bad?" Kari whispered. "Like is someone in trouble?"

Ashley shook her head. "You said it was about the trip. I think you're right." She grinned. "But come on . . . Mom and Dad never have bad news." Ashley giggled. "And if anyone was in trouble it would be me." She pumped her fist in the air. "And I'm definitely not in trouble. Not this week!"

Kari nodded. Yes, that was it. Whatever this meeting was about, everything was going to be okay. Ashley was right. They were headed for the beach tomorrow morning.

What could possibly be wrong?

8

The Awful, Unthinkable,
Really Bad News

ASHLEY

As everyone took a seat, a strange kind of quiet came over the family. Ashley looked around. Brooke and Kari, Erin and Luke, even their parents sat quietly. No one wanted to speak. It was as if everyone knew something was coming.

But what?

Finally their dad took a long breath and opened his mouth. "First, we're leaving at seven tomorrow morning." He smiled at them. "Everyone packed?"

Ashley's siblings nodded. She was the only one. Again. "Almost." She gave her father a weak smile. "Sorry. Time ran away with me."

"Got away from you." He did a hushed laugh. "Time got away from you."

"Right." Ashley gave a single nod. "That."

Their mom seemed a little rigid. She looked at their dad and her eyes got serious. "John . . ." That's all she said.

Just his name.

"Right." Dad took another deep breath. "So . . . we have some big news. I've been offered a job at a hospital in Bloomington, Indiana."

Ashley blinked. Indiana? How was her dad going to make that drive every day? She leaned forward. The eyes of her siblings grew wide and no one said a word.

Their mom crossed her arms. Her eyes got watery, like she was about to cry.

Just inside her chest, Ashley could feel her heart beating faster. Harder. She tried to speak, tried to think about how to ask the big question: Why would her father take a job so far away?

But her words wouldn't come.

Dad held his hands together. "I'll be working at a brand-new facility, and I'll be in charge of the emergency room. It's a wonderful opportunity." His smile seemed calm, like everything was normal.

Except it wasn't. Not at all.

Ashley raised her hand. Her question came before anyone actually called on her. "How long will it take you to drive there every day?"

Their dad's face went kind of blank. "That's what I'm trying to say, honey." He looked from her to Brooke and then to Kari and to Erin and finally Luke. "We're moving! To Indiana."

Mom took a deep breath. "At the end of the school year."

Ashley felt like she was on a spinning merry-go-round. One that wouldn't stop no matter what. This couldn't be happening. She raised her hand again. "The whole family?"

Kari was sitting beside her. She looked the way she had after the fall festival last year when she ate half her candy all at once. "You mean . . . we're leaving Ann Arbor?"

"We are." Their dad looked less happy than before. "I know this is a bit of a shock. But we'll be okay."

"What about school? And Lydia?" Ashley stood up. "I, for one, am not going. I'm not able to go. I already have a commitment here."

"Ashley." Their mom gave her a stern look. "Sit down, please. This is a family discussion. Not a protest." Her voice got softer. "Obviously we are not leaving anyone behind."

Ashley sat down. The spinning was getting worse.

"I'm fine with it." Brooke smiled at their dad. "The kids in my class are mean anyway. Something new is a great idea. New start. New everything."

New everything? Ashley sank back in her chair. No one could ever replace Lydia . . . or this house . . . or the skating rink down the street . . . or the way her mom looked making snickerdoodles in this exact kitchen after school.

Why would Brooke want something new?

Luke bounced a few times in his seat. "Will we get a big moving truck? Just like the Johnsons?"

"We will." Their dad seemed glad for Brooke's and Luke's responses. "What about you, Erin, honey?"

Ashley hadn't noticed Erin in all this. A quick look across the room at her sister and it was clear she wasn't happy or sad. Erin looked at their mom. "We'll all be together, right?"

"Of course." Mom gave Erin a very kind look. "No matter what."

"Okay, then." Erin's lips turned into the slightest smile. "That's all I care about."

Of course that was all Erin cared about. It was easier for her because she was only eight. Her whole life was this family and her books. Ashley crossed her arms. She loved her family as much as Erin did. And she loved this house. But she could not imagine leaving school and Ann Arbor. And she definitely couldn't stand the thought of leaving Lydia.

This was maybe the worst news ever.

Ashley tried to focus on what her parents were saying, but she couldn't. Something about packing up at the end of April and leaving the day after school got out.

For a second, she closed her eyes. When she opened them the room seemed like it was shrinking. Also her heartbeat sounded loud. She rubbed her sweaty palms on her jeans and tried to take a big breath. But she felt tired like after an hour of running around at recess or a whole soccer game.

All around her the people in her family were talking. Even Kari didn't look as sad as before. Ashley just wanted the meeting to stop, wanted everyone to go back to the details of the trip. So the meeting could be about the South Carolina beach.

But they kept talking. Which could only mean one thing. This was really happening.

They were moving.

"So what are the names of our new schools?" Brooke looked more excited all the time. "And what's the weather like in Indiana?"

"Can I play baseball there?" Luke raised his eyebrows high up his forehead.

"Yeah." Kari nodded. "And is there soccer?"

Ashley couldn't believe it. Her siblings had a million questions.

She only had one.

"Why?" She looked around the room. That's when her eyes filled with tears. "Why are you doing this?"

"We." Her father's look told her that the move was already a for-sure thing. "*We* are doing this. As a family." He seemed to relax a little. "Ashley, you're going to love it. We all are."

"What if *we* don't want to go?" Ashley didn't want to sound rude. But maybe it wasn't too late. Maybe her dad would understand that this was awful, unthinkable, really bad news.

Tears started spilling down Ashley's cheeks. Didn't anyone understand her? They had a deal, right? This was their home and they were never, ever leaving.

Dad only let out a long sigh and rubbed the back of his neck. At the same time, their mom stood and came to her. "Ashley . . . sweetheart, it'll be okay."

She sat next to Ashley and pulled her into her arms. Then she rocked her back and forth like she used to do when Ashley was little. "You can cry. I know it's not the news you expected."

"W-w-why are we moving?" Ashley's voice was small and sad. Tears crowded out her words. She rested her head on her mom's chest and wiped her cheeks.

The room was quiet again. Like everyone was watching her.

Ashley tried to find the bravest part of her heart. They were moving. There were no options. And she didn't like everyone watching her cry. She lifted her head and looked around.

Kari was crying, too. Silent tears, but still. At least she understood.

"Dad." Ashley still didn't understand. She brushed at her wet cheeks. "You already have a good job here. Why do you have to go to Indiana?"

Their dad leaned forward, elbows on his knees. "My job here was never permanent, sweetheart. Trust me. This is a much better position. The head doctor at a new hospital."

"What's the place again?" Ashley couldn't remember anything but Indiana. "Bloom Town?"

"Bloomington."

Bloomington. Ashley didn't like the sound of that. "Like where flowers bloom?" It sounded like a place covered with roses and tulips. Which might be boring. Besides, no place could ever be better than Ann Arbor. This was their home.

"I have a question." Two more tears slid down Kari's cheeks as she talked. "How far away is Bloomington?"

Their mom still had her arm around Ashley, but she leaned forward so she could see Kari better. "About six hours."

"Six hours." Ashley was on her feet again. "I'll never see Lydia again as long as I live."

"That's not true." Their dad's words were extra-warm. "We can take trips on the weekend to see Lydia. You can still be friends."

Ashley sat back down. Trips on the weekend? What about their lunch table? What about being snowflakes together?

"It really will be okay." Her mom brushed her hair back from her face. "I'm sorry, Ash."

"One thing." Kari sniffed. "I really do hope they have soccer."

"They will." Their dad seemed like he was trying to have pep in his voice. So the whole family would be happy. "And we'll still have each other."

Their mother nodded. "What do I always tell you kids?"

Erin was the first to answer. "Your very best friends are the ones sitting around the dining room table every night."

"Exactly." Mom nodded. "God will be with us. A year from now Bloomington will feel like home."

Ashley couldn't believe that would happen. Not in a year. Not ever. She felt tired in her soul. "Why did you tell us before the beach?" Her throat had a line of sobs ready to come out. "N-n-now the trip is ruined."

"Well . . ." Their mom wrapped her free arm around Kari, who was sitting on her other side. "Our Realtor is putting up the FOR SALE sign while we're gone." She looked at Brooke and Luke and Erin, and then at Kari. Finally she turned her eyes to Ashley. "We didn't want you to be surprised."

A FOR SALE sign? For this beautiful house? The one she'd been drawing just a half an hour ago? More tears filled up Ashley's eyes. So this *was* real. Not a scary dream.

And a Realtor? Well . . . Ashley wasn't quite sure what that was. But it didn't sound right. Nothing did. And something happened that she was not expecting. She didn't really care about the beach anymore.

She was too sad.

"I know moving isn't fun." Her father's voice was nice, like usual. And maybe extra-understanding. "It really is okay to be sad." Their father looked at each one of them again. "But God is calling us to Bloomington."

"He's calling *you* to Bloomington." Ashley crossed her arms. If her dad didn't take that job, they wouldn't be moving.

Her dad smiled. "True. He is. It is my job that's moving us. But I think everyone will benefit from the move. It's an opportunity to meet new people and make new memories. It's time to move on."

Their mom checked all the faces around her and then turned to their father. She sighed and stretched her arms wide. "Come on, kids. Come here." Ashley and Kari moved closer to their mom. Luke, Brooke, and Erin slowly crossed the room to her. They all piled onto the couch, like they often did.

One big family.

Her mom wrapped her arms around all five kids as best as she could and hugged them close.

Dad sat on the floor so he could look them all in the eyes, and then he took a breath. "We are the Baxter family. We will be okay. We have each other."

Deep down, maybe somewhere near her knees, Ashley knew her parents were right. They were going to be okay. They still had each other. But she didn't like it. And up high, near her heart, something was crumbling like a soup cracker.

Their dad clapped his hands, like Ashley's soccer coach sometimes did. "Come on. Everyone on your feet." He smiled, rallying the troops. "Let's pray."

Baxter family meetings always ended by talking out loud to God. Ashley stood, and so did the others. They got in a circle and bowed their heads.

"Dear God . . . we know this is hard. But we pray for strength and guidance as we plan our move . . ."

As her dad started praying, Ashley started words of her own. She had lots to say.

God. I'm kind of mad. I have that hurt feeling in my heart. I don't want to move. I like my school. I like Ann Arbor. I'm going to miss Lydia so much. I don't even know how I'm going to tell her. And I don't know anything about Bloomington. I want to stay here.

Help me believe that this will be okay. And help me have patience and keep breathing. I don't know what else to say. Just . . . help me get through the goodbyes.

Her dad was finishing his prayer. "And, God, help us get through the goodbyes."

Ashley popped her eyes open. She stared at her dad. How did he know that's what she had just asked God? Goose bumps ran down her arms. Maybe God really was here. She looked out the window to the still-winter sky. And just maybe He was listening.

Their dad closed by saying, "Please keep us safe at the beach and may we have a fun time together. As a family! In Jesus' name, amen!"

"Amen." Ashley and her siblings and their mom echoed their father and they squeezed each other's hands. Ashley felt a little bit better.

"Dinner is in thirty minutes." Their mom made her way to the kitchen.

Ashley looked at her siblings. And suddenly there was only one place they all wanted to go:

The tree house.

The Tree House

ASHLEY

Ashley was the first one to reach the back door. If ever there was a tree house day, it was this one.

Dad had built the tree house lots of years ago. It wasn't too far off the ground, and the main platform was held up by two big thick trees. But it had different levels to get up to the main one, the house part, which had walls and a roof. All five of them could fit inside. The tree house was their special place.

They had sleepovers in the tree house every summer, and game nights on the weekends. In autumn they drank cider there and told stories by flashlight. And sometimes on warm spring nights they stared at the stars through the opening in the roof.

But they also went to the tree house when something big was happening and they needed to talk it out. Like last fall, when Brooke was starting middle school all by herself.

Today was definitely tree house big.

They hurried into the backyard, toward the far corner. Most of the snow had melted, but the air was still freezing. While they ran, Ashley noticed everything she loved about the place. The hundred trees near the back fence and the spot where the tulips would line the porch later that spring.

And the tree house, of course. Especially that.

They all reached the spot and, without saying anything, they climbed from one platform to the next until they were on the main one. They sat down in a circle in silence. Nothing to say.

Their family was moving.

Brooke spoke first. "It's going to be fine. I really believe that." She put her hands in her sweatshirt pockets. "We have to trust Mom and Dad."

"I'm excited." Erin was playing with a stick. "But I'm scared, too. I don't want to make new friends."

Ashley watched Brooke reach across the circle and give Erin's hand a soft squeeze. "It's okay to be afraid. Even sad." Brooke kept her voice quiet. Times like this in the tree house they always talked quiet.

Brooke's kindness made Ashley's heart feel warm. They really did have each other. Next to her, Kari tilted her head back and looked up into the tree branches. Ashley felt sad for her. This was most hard on the two of them.

"You okay?" Ashley put her arm around Kari.

A hurt breath came from her. "I thought we would never move." Kari put her head on Ashley's shoulder. "Remember? We talked about it that day at the ice rink."

The others were watching, listening. Brooke put her arm around Erin, and Luke played with his shoelaces. Tying them. Untying them. Something he did when he was nervous.

Ashley leaned her head on Kari's. "It's not fair. I think we should get a vote." She looked at her siblings. "But we don't. It's happening."

Luke jumped up and crossed the circle to Ashley.

"You're going to be fine, Sissy." That was Luke's nick-name for her. Sissy. "Trust Mommy and Daddy."

"Thanks, Luke." Ashley hugged him.

Brooke and Erin and Kari joined them, and for a long minute all five of them stayed in a circle hug. The happiness from earlier that day seemed like a distant memory.

Ashley couldn't believe this was actually happening. It was real. Through the window of the tree house, she spotted the swing set their dad had built them a few years ago. And the garden where her mother grew carrots and zucchini in the summer.

A bin of basketballs and soccer balls sat on the back porch near Dad's grill. How would it look empty? After they moved away? New tears made Ashley's eyes blurry.

Lonely and sad, that's how.

Gradually Brooke and Erin and Luke took their seats in the circle again and the hug ended. Still everyone was quiet. Ashley closed her eyes, her shoulders hunched forward a little.

Everything was going to change, and there was nothing any of them could do about it.

This was their last spring in Ann Arbor.

"Dinner!" Their mother called from the back patio. Ashley watched her shade her eyes. "Come on, kids."

Brooke jumped up and looked out the window toward the house. "Coming." She yelled so Mom would hear her. "Two minutes, okay?"

"Okay." Their mother sounded happy. Like their whole world wasn't falling apart. "Hurry!"

Brooke took her place in the circle again. "Let's make a promise."

That sounded good. Ashley nodded. Luke and Erin and Kari did, too.

"Let's promise we'll find our own spot at our new house." Brooke looked from Kari to Luke, and then to Erin and finally Ashley. "And that we'll always remember."

"Remember what?" Luke sat up straighter. He definitely wanted to understand.

Ashley felt sorry for him. His blue eyes looked so young. He would probably barely remember Ann Arbor.

Brooke looked at him. "What's important. No

matter how lonely or sad it gets." She seemed to have thought this through. "Even if it's hard to make friends or find a new life in Bloomington . . . we always, always have each other. We have to promise to remember that."

Like a slow summer breeze, peace came over Ashley. "Yes." She nodded. This was the perfect promise.

"I like it." Kari nodded.

Erin did the same. "Me, too."

Luke's smile was quick and innocent. "If we have each other, that's all we need." He thought for a second. "And Mommy and Daddy. And God."

"Right, buddy." Brooke did a part laugh, part smile. "That *is* all we need."

Ashley put her hand in the middle, and her siblings did the same thing. This was something else the Baxter kids did often. It was how they made a promise.

Brooke said the words. "One . . . two . . . three . . ." And all at the same time they finished the promise. "Team!"

That was that. It was settled. No matter what,

they would help each through the move. Through whatever else was coming. They hurried inside and joined Mom and Dad setting the table for dinner.

Their mother smiled at Ashley. "Good meeting?"

"Yes." Ashley was still sad. But at least she had hope. She tried to give her mom the slightest smile. "The best."

But even though Ashley felt better than when Mom and Dad first made the announcement about the move, she and her siblings were still sad. Their dad tried to be chipper at dinner, but everyone was quiet.

Except Luke. He talked the whole time about sand castles and how his was going to be the biggest.

When they were finished eating, Dad looked around the table. "So who's excited for the beach?"

"Me." Brooke was the first to answer. Her lips lifted into an almost smile. "I think it'll be great." She looked at Kari, like she wanted her to say something.

"Yeah." Kari must have taken the hint. "Me, too." She found her prettiest smile for Brooke and then their father. "It's going to be great."

Ashley still wasn't sure. A week at the beach before saying goodbye to their whole world? Before a FOR SALE sign appeared in their grassy front yard?

"Ashley. What about you?" Her mom leaned her elbows on the table and looked straight at her.

"Um. Yeah." Ashley could feel everyone watching her. "The beach. Sure." Ashley picked up her fork and moved it through what was left of her mashed potatoes. "Who doesn't like the beach?" She felt the tears rushing up in her eyes, so she gave herself strict instructions. *Don't cry, Ashley. Don't cry.*

"Ashley." Her mom waited. "Honey, it's okay to cry. We talked about that."

Ashley tried not to, but nothing worked. Her tears came anyway. She was crying. And everyone could see.

"One good thing." Luke smiled at her. He had love and care in his face. "It's probably more fun to be sad at the beach than here." He looked around. "At least it'll be warm."

His words hit Ashley all at once. And suddenly

she did something she didn't expect. Something that felt perfect and wonderful.

She laughed.

Then Kari laughed and Erin and Brooke. Luke, too. And finally their parents joined in. And all the sudden there they were, the whole family laughing like the whole world wasn't falling apart. Like they weren't moving away from all they knew and loved and wanted.

Laughter was the best cure, and as they cleared the table Ashley thought just maybe, she might live through the move.

But later that night, when the lights were out and Kari was sleeping, Ashley couldn't find a way to be tired. She stared at her ceiling and then out the window at the dark night sky.

She thought about Lydia and all the adventures they would never have, and in a small flood the tears came back. This time there was no reason not to cry. Luke wasn't here to make her laugh, and no one was watching. She rolled onto her stomach and cried the way she had wanted to ever since she heard the terrible news.

Ashley didn't hear her mother walk in but all the sudden she was sitting on the bed beside her.

"I know you're still upset about the move." Her mom's voice was soft and quiet. And maybe something else. Maybe a little sad.

A quick look and Ashley felt the shock hit her. There were tears in her mom's eyes, too. "Mom." Ashley sat up a little bit. "It's okay to cry."

Her mom laughed and wiped at her tears. "Thanks."

"Why are *you* sad?" Ashley sat up and held the pillow to her stomach. "You seemed happy to move."

"Sweetheart . . ." Her mom took her hand. "This is our home. We've been here since we brought Kari home from the hospital." She looked around the room. "So many memories live in these walls." She closed her eyes for a short moment. "I don't *want* to leave. Your dad doesn't, either."

"But how come . . ." Ashley didn't finish the sentence.

"Dad has an amazing opportunity, that's why." Her mother nodded, very sure. "I will always support him. We all need to do that." She smiled even as another tear fell onto her cheek. "I trust God that what's ahead will be even better than what's here."

Ashley lay back down. A million questions zipped around her mind. But she understood something now. The move was hard even for her parents. She hadn't thought of that before.

"Yes, that's it. I need to trust God." Ashley dried her eyes and looked right at her mom. "I'll try."

"And I'll help. Whenever you're sad." Mom bent down and kissed her forehead. "Remember, honey. God loves you even more than we do. He won't let you down."

"Okay." Ashley yawned. "Can you rub my back? Please." Ashley turned onto her tummy again. She was starting to feel better.

Her mom rubbed her back and hummed a song. Something they'd sung in church before. "Great Is Thy Faithfulness." She didn't know all the words, but she could tell it was that song from the melody. She liked how the song made her feel. Peaceful and calm.

Like everything was going to be okay. Not because it would be easy. But because they had each other. And their very best friends weren't the ones at school. Not here or in Bloomington.

They were the ones around the dining room table.

10

The Beach and the Boy

KARI

Kari couldn't imagine a car ride taking longer than this one.

They had been driving since dark that morning. Turned out, the drive from Michigan to South Carolina was fourteen hours long.

But it felt like a million years.

"The road trip is part of the adventure." Their dad looked in the rearview mirror and grinned. He'd been saying that all day. But Kari and the other kids were beginning to wonder.

Already they had played music and I Spy and License Plate Bingo. They were two hours from the beach and it seemed the only thing left to do was sleep or read. Kari was just ready to be at the ocean!

She adjusted her pillow against the car door and closed her eyes. When she opened them they were parked at a grocery store. Their dad must've gone inside for food. Kari leaned forward. "Are we close?"

Her mom nodded. "Just a few minutes away."

"Yes!" She couldn't wait to be on the beach.

Their dad returned with three bags of groceries and put them in the back, just as the other kids woke up. "Here we go." Their dad grinned at them. "Next stop—the beach house!"

The whole car burst into shouts of joy and some applause. As their dad drove, Kari paid attention to the road. Sidewalks became sandy paths, and then she noticed more cars pulling boats. She began to see beach houses, brightly colored and inviting. And then . . . Kari spotted it!

"The ocean! Look!" Kari tugged at Ashley's shirt.

Ashley was still sort of sleepy. But now she sat up straight. "It's beautiful!" Her eyes got big.

The rest of the car began buzzing about the beach and the water and the sun and all the things they were going to do.

Finally, they pulled into a driveway, and a beautiful house sat on a sandy hill in front of them. Kari gasped.

Her dad unbuckled his seat belt and turned to the kids. "We're here!"

"It's perfect!" Kari stepped out of the car and stared at the house. It was a two-story yellow house with gigantic windows.

The other kids got out of the car and ran with her around the house to the beach side.

"A balcony!" Ashley raised both hands like this was a big victory. "I love balconies."

They helped their parents bring in the groceries, and Kari and her sisters ran through the house discovering every room. The side of the house facing the beach was almost entirely windows.

Which meant they could see the ocean from everywhere they looked.

Their mom met them in the living room. "Come on." She grinned. "I'll show you your rooms."

The one downstairs was for her and their dad, she told them. "Let's go upstairs."

Luke joined them, and all five kids followed

Mom up a long staircase. Like at home Kari and Ashley shared a room, but this time Brooke was in with them, too. Kari was glad. She loved spending time with Brooke.

"Bunk beds. Cool!" Ashley threw her pillow on the higher bunk. "I call top!"

Kari laughed. "Fine with me. I like sleeping closer to the floor."

Another room at the end of the hallway was for Luke and Erin. Kari had an idea. "Let's unpack our suitcases first."

"Wait!" Ashley had stepped into the hallway. Now she poked her head into the girls' room. "I found something!"

They filed into the hallway, and Luke and Erin and Mom joined them. Ashley pointed to a spiral staircase right across from Luke and Erin's room. Kari had never seen a real spiral staircase. It was like something from a fairy tale!

"Let's go up!" Kari made the first move, and at the top she stepped into the most amazing lookout! It was like a small room with windows all the way around.

"Wow!" Ashley's feet froze on the floor. Like it was too special to take in all at once. "This is the best ever."

"It's like our tree house." Luke ran to the window and looked out. "Only it's a real house with real windows."

Brooke joined Luke. "The view!"

"It's amazing!" Erin stood by their mom.

Kari and Ashley were speechless. The view was one of the most beautiful things Kari had ever seen. She could tell Ashley was thinking the same thing.

"Hey, look." Ashley pointed down below. "Neighbors!"

Kari saw what Ashley was looking at. A family was moving things into the home next door. They were unloading their car, talking and laughing.

"Looks like two kids." Ashley sounded happier than she had all day. "Our same age! See! I told you Hilton Head has lots of kids."

Kari shrugged. New kids weren't on her mind much. Like she'd told Ashley yesterday, this trip was for family.

Next they unpacked and helped their mom and

dad put away groceries. Then they kicked off their shoes and changed into their bathing suits and cover-ups and the whole family walked down to the beach.

"This is the warmest spring break in a decade." Their dad turned his face to the sun. "It's going to be a perfect week!"

He added that the water would still be cold since it was only late March. But it would probably be warm enough to play in the waves.

"I can't wait to put my feet in the surf." Ashley sounded a lot happier than she had last night. Kari watched her run ahead. Luke kept up with her.

Kari took her time. She skimmed her hand along the tall grass lining the path and stopped to smell some little white flowers. The sound of the waves felt like it was healing her heart, helping her better understand the fact that her family was moving.

On either side of them, tall palm trees stretched to the sky. Kari loved them. *God must have had fun creating the beach*, she thought. *Everything is so perfect.*

After a few minutes at the water's edge, Mom and Dad went back inside with Luke and Erin.

Time to make dinner, Mom told them. Erin and Luke were going to help.

But Kari really knew what Mom was doing. She didn't want the youngest two near the water without supervision. Kari remembered. That was how it used to be with her and Ashley and Brooke when they were little.

When it was just the three girls, Kari had watched the waves roll up onto the shore one after another. They were actually here at the beach! She followed Ashley down to the wet sand. Brooke came, too. They ran into the surf, splashing and laughing.

Yes, the ocean water was cold, but with the sun on their faces it felt great.

"I'll get the paddleball set!" Kari ran up the sand to the back porch. Ashley and Brooke were still in the water, but only up to their knees.

When Kari returned with the paddles, Ashley joined her on the warm sand. Not far away, Brooke stretched out on her towel with a book.

"Here we go." Kari handed Ashley a paddle and they began to volley the ball back and forth.

"Do you think Dad will grill hot dogs tomorrow night?" Ashley hit the ball to Kari. But she must have hit it way too hard, because the ball sailed over Kari's head out to the water.

"Oh no!" Kari ran into the waves.

Just then a voice yelled behind her. "Look out!" Kari turned, but it was too late. She got knocked into the water. At the same time a wave crashed over her and suddenly the boy from next door was helping her to her feet.

"Sorry." He had a Frisbee in his hand. "I didn't see you."

Kari was drenched. She let go of his hand and wiped the salt water from her eyes. She spit a piece of seaweed from her mouth. "It's . . . okay. Accidents happen."

Brooke and Ashley ran up. Brooke looked really worried. "You okay?"

"Yes." A shiver ran over Kari. Her teeth started clattering. "J-j-just freezing."

"Wow." The neighbor boy looked upset. "I'm really sorry."

Kari figured the boy was about her age. He ran

up the sand and grabbed his towel. Then he ran it back to Kari. "Here. Use this." He stepped away. "I'm Braden. Looks like we're neighbors this week." He studied Kari. "You sure you're okay?"

"Yes." The towel helped. Kari pulled it more tightly around herself.

The girl from next door walked up. Braden looked at her and then at Kari and Brooke. "This is my older sister, Lilly."

Kari smiled. "This is *my* older sister, Brooke." The neighbor kids seemed very nice. "I'm Kari."

Lilly turned to Brooke. "I like your swimsuit!"

Brooke smiled. "Thanks! I like yours, too. I have an extra towel and some magazines if you wanna sit with me?"

"Yeah! Of course." Lilly seemed thrilled.

Braden grinned at Kari. "Wanna play Frisbee?"

Ashley stepped up and made a coughing sound. "I'm Ashley. The other sister." She held her hand out to Braden.

He shook it. "So . . . how old are you all?"

"I'm in fourth grade." Ashley tilted her chin up. Clearly proud of the fact. "What about you?"

"I'm in sixth." He looked at Kari. "What about you?"

"Fifth." Kari liked these kids. "Where are you from?"

Kari looked over at Ashley, who seemed to be getting upset that she wasn't being noticed. But Kari didn't think it was her fault. For some reason, Braden seemed more interested in talking to her, and not to Ashley.

"We're from Ohio." He squinted at Kari again, the sun on his face. "So . . . what about Frisbee?"

"Sure." Kari dried off some more. She looked at Ashley. They had just started their paddleball game, after all. "Is that okay?"

Ashley looked frustrated, but she shrugged. "I guess."

Brooke and Lilly headed for the towels up the beach. Ashley took both paddles and the ball and turned toward the house. "I'm going in."

"Don't you want to play Frisbee?" Kari started after her.

"No." Ashley looked over her shoulder. "I don't like Frisbee."

Braden watched her go. Then he smiled at Kari. "I guess it's us two."

They played Frisbee for half an hour, until Kari's mom called them in for dinner. Kari couldn't believe how much fun the new kids were. Who would've thought she'd be friends with the neighbor boy so quickly?

Later, when the whole family was seated at the table, Brooke shared her news. "I met a new friend named Lilly. She's our neighbor and she's super nice."

"Me, too." Kari felt even happier about the coming week. "His name is Braden. He's great at Frisbee."

"Please." Ashley rolled her eyes. "He almost hurt you! Boys are always knocking girls over. All because of sports."

"What happened?" Their dad looked concerned.

Kari explained the story and Ashley didn't say anything else. After dinner the family went out back to play games on the beach.

Not long after, the kids from next door joined in. Braden brought a soccer ball and everyone played.

Everyone but Ashley.

She and Erin stayed to themselves playing paddleball a long way from the rest of the group. Kari
made a note to talk to Ashley later. Until then she
was having the time of her life. The beach . . . the
warm air . . . the ocean waves and her family.

And a new friend.

Which taught Kari something that made her
heart happy. Maybe moving to Bloomington
wouldn't be that bad, after all.

11

Being Invisible

ASHLEY

It was turning out to be the worst trip ever, as far as Ashley was concerned. It was just before lunch on day three and she was about to build a sand castle with Erin. Again.

The problem was the kids next door.

Ever since the first day, when that Braden boy crashed into Kari, and that Lilly became best friends with Brooke, Ashley had become invisible. At least it seemed that way based on how Brooke and Kari were acting.

This morning she even stood in front of the mirror to see if she really was invisible. But her arms and legs and face were right there in the glass on the bathroom wall. So it must just be that her sisters couldn't see her.

"What are we building today?" Erin had found five sand buckets and an array of yellow and blue plastic shovels in the downstairs closet. She sat beside Ashley. "Another sand castle?"

"I guess." Ashley tried to smile. It wasn't Erin's fault. "Let's make it taller than yesterday."

"Maybe like a city building." Erin's eyes lit up. "Instead of a castle."

Ashley patted her younger sister's hand. "That might be fun." Erin was still so little. Spending time with her was the best part of being ignored by Brooke and Kari.

Definitely, Ashley was trying to find the silver cloud here.

Or something like that.

Their mom and Luke joined Ashley and Erin. Mom had a big red beach bag full of lunch for whenever someone got hungry. Ashley watched her mom set up her beach chair. She adjusted her sunglasses and sunhat and opened a book.

Luke ran up and slid into the spot on the other side of Ashley. "I'll help. What are we building?"

"A castle." Ashley looked from Luke to Erin. "Made of sand."

"Or a city building . . . Hi, Luke!" Erin looked even happier than before. "You can help, too!" She handed him a plastic rake and he got to work.

"I have a busy schedule today." Luke looked over his shoulder as he flattened the sand in front of them. "Me and Dad are going snorgling."

"Snorgling?" Ashley wrinkled her nose. She looked at her mom. "What's snorgling?"

"Snorkeling." Her mom glanced up from her book, her eyes happy. "Your brother is going to learn how to snorkel."

"That's right." Luke hesitated mid-effort with the sand rake. "I always forget. Snorkel. Snorkel. Snorkel." He giggled. "Sounds like a seal laughing."

Ashley figured that was as good a way to remember it as any. A seal laughing.

Their mother put her hand above her eyes. "Where're Kari and Brooke?"

Ashley pointed down the beach. Her sisters

were on tubes, floating and laughing with Braden and Lilly. "Over there." Ashley rolled her eyes and looked back at the sand field in front of her. "Having the time of their lives."

"Hmm." Mom set her book down and looked at Ashley. "Didn't they have another tube?"

"No. Just four. All week there's been only four of everything." Ashley lifted her chin. "It's fine. I'm not sad. I don't want to play with them, anyway."

Her mother's voice was gentle in the ocean air. "Well I'm sure it's not intentional, sweetheart."

Ashley raised one shoulder and dropped it again. "Whatever. I'm fine." This wasn't the time to talk about it. She was trying to be happy, so she smiled.

"Okay, then. If you say so." Her mom's voice told Ashley there would be more conversation about this later. When Erin and Luke weren't around.

Mom knew everything, so she definitely knew Ashley would have more fun out in the ocean with the big kids. But that wasn't going to happen, so they both dropped the subject.

Now Dad came around the corner of the house

headed their way. "Beautiful day at the beach!" He was always happy, whether he was in the waves or on the sand.

Ashley tried to learn a lesson from him. But she wasn't the best student on days like this.

"Time for snorgling!" Luke jumped up and ran to their dad. Midway he stopped and did a single laugh. "Not snorgling." He scratched his head. "Oh! Snor-kel-ing. That's it. Snorkel. Snorkel. Snorkel." His laughter made the afternoon feel a little lighter.

That's why Luke was one of Ashley's favorite people.

Dad set up a chair next to Mom and all five of them ate lunch.

"If you could be any ocean animal, which would you want to be?" Ashley's dad took a bite of his sandwich and looked out at the ocean. He was always asking them questions like this.

"I think I'd be a clown fish!" Luke was the first to find an answer. He was pretty funny, so a clown fish made the most sense.

Ashley furrowed her brow and pursed her lips. Her imagination ran wild. If she could be *any* ocean animal . . . ? There were too many to name just one.

"I think I'd like to be a sea horse." Her mom took a sip of her iced tea. "What about you, Ash?"

"This is a tough question." Ashley grabbed a handful of chips. "But, I think I'd have to pick a dolphin. They seem the most friendly."

"That's perfect for you." Ashley's dad finished up his lunch and winked at her. "Because you're the most friendly Ashley I know." He wadded up his napkin and put it in the trash bag. Ashley turned back to the waves and smiled. She liked hearing that. It made her feel better about being left out by her sisters.

Ashley's eyes found the spot along the shore where her sisters were still having fun with the neighbor kids, and she felt sad again. She wanted to be with her older sisters. They looked like they were having the best vacation ever.

After lunch, Ashley and Erin and Luke worked on the castle, but before they were half done, Luke set his shovel down and jumped up. "I'm ready to snor-kel." He grinned at their dad. "Can we go now?"

"Excellent idea, Luke-ster!" Their dad dug through their mom's beach bag and pulled out two snorkels. He gave Luke an adventure type of smile. "Now's the perfect time!" He stood and handed one of the snorkels to Luke.

"Can I go?" Ashley looked up at her dad. She wouldn't be left behind again, right?

"Oh." He frowned. "Ash, we only brought two snorkels. I'm sorry. Maybe after Luke, you can have a turn."

"Okay. . ." She slumped down into the sand. This day was not going her way. Only four floating water tubes. Only two snorkels. She looked at Erin. Her little sister was still happy, filling a castle mold with sand. Nothing ever bothered her.

Ashley sighed. If only she could be more like Erin.

After Dad and Luke walked toward the water, her mom stood, too, and approached Ashley and Erin. She put her hand on Ashley's shoulder. "You okay?"

"Yes." Ashley brushed some sand off her nose and began filling a pail. "No big deal."

Her mom patted her head. "You sure?"

"I'm sure." Ashley looked up at her mom, then at her sister. "We're going to build the best sand castle in the whole world. Right, Erin?"

"That's right." Erin smoothed out the spot where the first part of the castle was coming to life. "Best castle on the whole beach."

Whole *beach*? Ashley blinked. That didn't have quite the same ring as best in the world. She laughed a little. "Sure. Okay. Whatever." Her laugh felt good. First one in a lot of hours. "The world. The beach. As long as it's the best."

"It will be." Erin stopped and patted Ashley on her back. "Don't worry." She grinned. "Being happy is a choice." She looked at their mother. "Right, Mom?"

"It is." Their mom was still watching them. She sat back in her beach chair and smiled at Erin. "I like how you think, honey." She shifted her eyes to Ashley. "Sometimes you have to choose happiness. Your whole day gets better when you do."

"That settles it." Ashley smiled at Erin. "These happy sisters are going to get this castle built!"

Ashley and Erin spent the rest of the afternoon building the greatest sand castle creation Ashley had ever seen. It had three tall towers, pretty seashell decorations, pathways and a bunch of doors. They even made a moat around it with a bridge from the world to the castle entrance.

Like something from a fairy tale.

When they were finished, Ashley stood and surveyed their work. "Pretty impressive." She put her arm around Erin's shoulders. They were both covered in sand and worn out from the effort.

But the time spent was worth it.

"See?" Erin grinned at Ashley and then at their mom, who was still reading in her chair. "Look, Mom! It's perfect."

Their mom stood and studied the castle and right away her eyes got impressed. "Girls! It's incredible." She grabbed her camera from her beach bag. "Okay, kneel next to your castle."

Ashley and Erin did as they were told, arms around each other while their mother took the picture. Then Erin turned to Ashley. Her eyes sparkled, like she was about to do something crazy. "Now let's knock it down and start again! Before the waves do!"

Ashley raised her eyebrows. She could feel her face get full of question marks. She had never seen this side of Erin. "I like the way you think." Ashley nodded. "Yes! Three . . . Two . . . one . . ."

"Go!" Erin knocked over the first tower with a shout.

Ashley and Erin were having fun kicking up sand. Their mom got a few funny photos of them. Something they could laugh at later when they remembered this day.

"I'm a dinosaur! Rawwwwr!" Ashley stomped on the foundation of the castle.

Erin giggled. "Me too!" She stomped on another section and growled.

This was actually super fun!

When dino demolition was over, and the castle was just a bunch of sand again, the girls sat there. Quiet. This day didn't turn out so bad, after all. Erin was little, but she was a lot of fun. Which was actually a new thought for Ashley.

Plus, she had chosen to be happy like Erin and

that had worked out. Because happy was who Ashley was deep down inside. And being happy was being true to herself.

Also, sometimes the best times are unexpected times.

Ashley and Erin moved their towels next to their mom's chair. She handed them each an apple and the three of them sat there staring at the beach. Brooke and Kari and the neighbor kids were still playing in the waves. Dad was still snorkeling with Luke.

But none of them had the thrill of pretending to be a dinosaur while leveling a whole entire sand castle.

"I have an idea." Their mom leaned back and looked at the sky. A million puffy white clouds drifted over the beach. Mom grinned at Ashley and Erin and then looked up again. "Let's see what we can find in the clouds."

Ashley loved this game. She leaned back and stared at the clouds. Just then she saw something. "There. That one's a car." Ashley pointed up. "See the tires? And over there's a centipede. Look at those legs!"

"I see it." Her mom sounded excited. This was another thing Ashley loved about their mother. She knew how to pretend.

"I see a tree!" Erin pointed a few clouds over. "See it? The branches are super enormous."

"They are!" Ashley loved this. "God's the best artist." She saw another one. "There's a castle. Just like the one we built."

Their mother laughed. "You're the sweetest girls." She turned soft eyes to Ashley and then to Erin. "I love you both so much."

"Love you, too." Ashley and Erin both said it.

And it occurred to Ashley that on this afternoon—even while missing out on tubing or snorkeling, and wishing she could be there—fun was right in front of her. She just had to pay attention to find it.

They really did have the best beach day of all. Erin and Ashley hadn't missed out. Because they had made a choice for happiness. Which was something Ashley was going to remember.

Because lots of days, you just needed to make that choice.

12

Choosing Happy

ASHLEY

That night Ashley wanted to sketch a bit. Drawing made her feel happy and calm. Like maybe God had created her to draw the way He created some people to dance or sing.

She found her new journal in her suitcase and took it out onto the upstairs back deck. Then she found a quiet spot with a view of the whole ocean and she turned to an open page. Today she would sketch two things.

A sand castle bigger than anything on the beach.

And a cloud shaped like a tree.

For a long time she sat there drawing. When she was finished she smiled at her work. *Perfect*, she thought. Just how she saw it in her heart. She sniffed the air. Her dad was grilling chicken for dinner and it smelled like home and vacation all mixed together.

"Dad." She ran down the stairs and found him standing at the grill. "Your chicken smells professional." She tucked her journal under her arm and smiled at him. "How do you do that?"

"Hi there." He laughed and closed the lid of the grill. "It's all in the marinating." He winked at Ashley and they took chairs beside each other.

Just then Brooke and Kari came up the sand, laughing and talking.

"Hi!" Kari waved at them. "We had the most fun day!"

Ashley looked down at the journal on her lap. She rolled her eyes. Never mind her own great day. She wasn't going to tell Brooke and Kari. They didn't care about her news, anyway. Not when they had ignored her all day.

Kari didn't seem to notice Ashley's hurt feelings. Ashley watched her carry a pail full of seashells. She couldn't stop talking about their great time. "After we played in the waves, we walked the whole beach and picked up the prettiest shells." She stared into her bucket. "But we never found a single sand dollar."

She held the pail up for Dad and Ashley to see.

Ashley crossed her arms and huffed. "No one cares about your shells."

Her dad gave her a look. "Ashley!"

She put her hand over her mouth. "Sorry." She hadn't actually meant for those words to cross from her heart over her lips. They were supposed to be for her insides only.

Her dad looked more hurt than angry. "That wasn't very nice. Your sisters are excited about their shells."

Tears were starting to come again. Ashley turned to her sisters. "I didn't mean it." She ordered her tears to stop. "It's just . . . you two left me out all day. Every day."

"You could've joined us anytime." Brooke's answer came quick.

Kari just looked down at the pail of shells. Like maybe she felt a little bad.

"We never left you out." Brooke's tone was impatient. "So don't pout about it now."

"I'm not pouting." Ashley stood and stared at Brooke. "You're being mean."

"Girls!" Their dad wasn't having any more of this. His tone made that clear. "That's enough."

Ashley couldn't stay another minute. She held her journal tight and ran back upstairs. Once inside the house, she raced down the hallway to the spiral staircase.

If ever she needed her tree house it was now. But the rooftop lookout would have to do.

She sat on the little sofa. The beach was spread out like a painting and the clouds hung over her like an umbrella. Now that she was alone, Ashley couldn't stop the tears.

This wonderful happy day was all ruined. Tears ran down her cheeks and onto her lips. They tasted salty and her heart felt heavy.

Words filled her soul and stayed there.

God, I feel so left out. All day I tried to be happy, but now . . . now I need help.

Sometimes she wished God would answer her out loud. Like maybe He could just sort of show up beside her and He could pat her head and tell her everything was going to be okay.

Ashley waited.

When that didn't happen, she had another idea. She stood and opened the windows. All six of them. She breathed in big so that the air filled her whole lungs. Then she sat back down and closed her eyes. *Are you there, God?* The sound of the ocean waves filled the little room.

Yes. Ashley could feel God all around her. He was here. She was sure of it.

A few more tears ran down her face.

That wasn't nice of Brooke and Kari. To desert her, and then brag about their shells. Rude. She hesitated. *What am I supposed to do, God?*

Choose to be happy.

Ashley opened her eyes. Was that God talking to her? Choose to be happy? Was that what He wanted her to do? She thought about that for a few minutes until she knew for sure.

Yes. That's what God wanted. Just like earlier. She needed to decide to be happy. Even if Brooke and Kari didn't ever include her the whole trip.

The sun was setting, spraying rays of light over the water. Ashley dried her cheeks and turned to a fresh page in her lined journal. There was something wonderful about a blank page. Even one with lines on it. Like God was giving her a new page in her heart, too.

Ashley began to draw.

She made a long line starting from the left side of the page to the right. The edge of the ocean. Little by little she filled in the water with waves and fish and a pair of dolphins, the kind of dolphin she wanted to be. Free and able to swim wherever they wanted and never get left out of anything. Then Ashley made a half circle above the water and sketched the sun rays coming out of it. She did a few clouds as well. One looked like a centipede.

Perfect.

She exhaled. Much better. She hated running away from everyone. Same way she had done the other night when they found out

151

about the move. She looked at the sky. "I really have been going through a lot here, God." She whispered the words out loud so God would be sure to hear them. "Any help would be greatly depreciated."

She heard a noise behind her and turned around. "Daddy! You scared me."

"Appreciated, Ashley. It's appreciated. Not depreciated." Her dad gave her a sad smile. "Mind if I sit?"

"No." She wiped her nose. "Go ahead."

"How do you feel?" He faced her.

"Better." She still had her journal open. She held up her drawing. "I made this."

"Wow." Her father took the book and studied her artwork. "You're very talented, Ashley." He looked really impressed. "One day people will pay money for your work. I believe that."

The compliment was like a gift straight to Ashley's heart. She closed the book and looked at her dad. "Really?"

"Definitely."

She smiled. "Thanks."

Now her dad took a slow breath. "How your sisters spent the day"—his words were soft—"they weren't trying to leave you out." His smile had the truest kindness. "They were just having fun."

"They only thought about themselves." Ashley looked back at the waves.

"Maybe." Her dad put his hand on her shoulder. "But they do love you very much. You know that."

Ashley let that thought hang in her head for a few seconds. Then she nodded. "I know. They do love me."

"Always remember that, Ash." Dad stood and held his hand to her. "Come on. Time for dinner."

The way her hand felt in his was safe and warm and good.

When they reached the long table in the dining room, Ashley walked over to Brooke and Kari. "I'm sorry." She smiled. Her eyes were still a little wet, but she felt a lot better. "I really did have the best day with Mom and Erin."

Everyone else was still setting the table, so the

three girls had this minute to work things out. Kari set down a pair of forks. Then she turned and hugged her. "We didn't mean to leave you out."

"I know." Ashley smiled. She was choosing happiness. Like God had reminded her. "We all do that sometimes."

Brooke hugged her next. "I'm sorry."

"It's okay." She pointed to the bucket on the table in the next room. "And later tonight, I want you to show me your shells!"

After dinner, they had a bonfire with s'mores. Braden and Lilly's family joined them, and everyone had a good time. Ashley was surprised that the family next door also loved to laugh and sing campfire songs. They were friendly.

But they didn't seem as close as Ashley's family. She wasn't sure why. After her kind of day, Ashley was grateful for a family who stayed close because they talked through hurt feelings. Not every family had those talks. But she would do everything she could to make sure the Baxters always did.

That night when the lights were off in the room

154

she shared with Brooke and Kari, Ashley thanked God for helping her feel better. *Happiness really is a choice, God. I get that now. Great is Your faithfulness. Just like the song.*

Just then Kari whispered from the bottom bunk. "Ashley?"

"Yes." Ashley lowered her face over the edge. She kept her voice quiet so she wouldn't wake up Brooke.

Kari smiled up at her. "Love you."

Everything felt right again. Ashley smiled back at her sister. "Love you, too."

As she fell asleep Ashley's heart was full. She thought about the fun time with Erin and her mom, stomping on the sand castle and staring at the clouds. Also the way things had worked out with Brooke and Kari. And something else.

Ashley no longer felt invisible.

She felt loved.

13

The Sand Dollar

KARI

Kari still hadn't found a sand dollar on the beach, and it was the last day of spring break. A sand dollar was the one thing she wanted to bring home. She made a decision to look later, before they packed up.

But first it was time to shop for souvenirs! After breakfast they piled into the car and headed to town. They were each allowed one thing—a hat or a T-shirt. A necklace. Something small as a keepsake from their trip.

At the store they met up with Braden and Lilly's family and all of them shopped together. The dads and Braden picked out T-shirts, but Luke wanted a baseball cap.

"Because I always have chicken hair." He laughed. It was how their mother described Luke's hair first thing in the morning. Or when he forgot to comb it.

All four girls and Lilly picked out shell necklaces. Each of them was beautiful and different.

"Because you're all unique," Kari's mom said when she looked at their choices. "No two of you are the same. That's good to remember."

Kari liked that. She would remember her mom's words whenever she wore her shell necklace.

Next the two families went to the arcade. It was on a sunny stretch of the street next to five more souvenir stores. Dad gave them each three dollars. "That's for six games."

He and Mom sat at a table with Braden and Lilly's parents, who said something about being ready to go home. Dad seemed ready, too. But only because he was excited for his new job.

The only thing good about Bloomington, so far.

Dad waved to them as they headed for the games. "Have fun!"

Braden and Lilly, Brooke, Erin and Luke all ran

to the Skee-Ball. But Kari had a different idea. She grinned at Ashley. "Let's play Pac-Man!"

"Perfect." Ashley ran for the nearest machine and Kari followed.

Pac-Man was the best game. Kari loved the way her heart raced when the little monsters chased her yellow guy. And then how they ran away when she swallowed up the big dots. Pac-Man was definitely her favorite.

But three rounds later Kari was losing to Ashley and ready for something else. She spotted the air hockey table at the other end of the arcade. "How about air hockey!"

"You sure you want to lose again?" Ashley laughed, her eyebrow raised.

Kari stuck out her chin and giggled. "Game on!" She loved that everything was good between them again.

The two of them ran to the air hockey table and grabbed their strikers.

"You start." Ashley slid the puck Kari's way. "I'll go easy on you. At least at first." Ashley spun her striker on the tabletop.

"Let's do this!" Kari hit the puck toward Ashley. She was determined to win. But a minute later she was down by two goals.

"I call winner." Braden came up behind Kari.

She stopped the puck and turned around. Her heart was still racing from the game. "Hi." She smiled. "You'll be playing Ashley, unless I can score."

Braden laughed. "I'll cheer for you." He took a chair a few feet away so he could watch.

"What about me?" Ashley put her hands on her hips. "You better cheer for me, too."

"I would"—Braden looked like he was enjoying this—"but you don't seem to need a lot of help, Ashley."

"True." Kari made a silly face. "Come on. I'm ready to score here." She slid the puck to Ashley and the game was back in motion. Soon enough they were tied. Game point.

"You got this, Kari." Braden was on his feet.

Kari felt her confidence rise. A jolt of encouragement was just what she needed. Ashley served the puck and they hit it back and forth. *Whack!* Kari hit the puck to Ashley's side, it curved alongside the wall and slowed down.

Thwap! Ashley hit it back to Kari. *"Aha!"*

The puck came zooming toward her. Kari's eyes locked on it as it bounced from one side to the other. She hit it hard, one last time. The puck flew across the table, a seamless, perfect line toward the goal, and slid straight into the slot.

"Yes! *Score!*" Kari threw her hands up. "I won!"

"No!" Ashley collapsed on the table. Always dramatic. "I call rematch!"

"Nice, Kari!" Braden high-fived her and made his way over to Ashley. "No rematch, sorry. I play winner."

"Fine." Ashley looked tired. But she didn't seem to care too much that she'd lost. She handed her striker to Braden. "I surrender."

He took it and slid the puck toward Kari. His eyes made her feel like they'd been friends for a long time. "Here we go!"

Whack!

A thought occurred to Kari as the game began. She would always remember this spring break. And a neighbor boy who in just a week became one of her favorite friends.

Early the next morning, Kari and her family packed up their things, and then the kids ran down to play in the surf one last time. Everyone but Kari. Instead, she pulled up a chair next to her mom in the shade and sat down. Kari was too sunburned to be in the water.

Her mom looked up from the book she was reading. "Kari, your poor cheeks. They're still so red." She smiled. "Glad you're staying out of the sun."

"It's for the best." Kari could feel that her smile wasn't her biggest. She'd rather be in the ocean. But being here with her mom was best this time. She stared down the beach. The other kids looked like they were getting tired. Wrapping towels around themselves.

"Such a great trip." Mom took a relaxed breath. "Seems like everyone's ready to get back home."

Kari wasn't so sure. There would be a FOR SALE sign in their grass when they pulled up. No one wanted to see that. She turned and looked next door. Braden and Lilly were packing up their towels and beach chairs. "I think I'll go say goodbye to the neighbors."

"Okay." Her mom looked back at her book. "Don't go far. We're leaving soon."

Kari nodded and set off. Her heart felt heavy and a little sad. She really liked Braden and Lilly. She wasn't ready to say goodbye. Up on the road she heard Braden's dad yell for the kids. "Braden . . . Lilly. Time to go!"

So far neither of them had noticed Kari walking up. But now Braden turned and saw her. He set down the two chairs he was carrying. "Hey."

"Hey." Kari looked up the hill for Lilly. "You're leaving?"

"Yeah. In a few hours." Braden squinted in the bright sunlight. "Long trip ahead."

"Us, too. My dad's loading up the car." Kari grinned and did a little shrug. "It's been fun."

"The best." He looked like he wasn't sure what to say. "Maybe we'll see each other again here. Some spring break."

"Maybe." Kari saw Lilly walk out the back door of their house. She ran down the hill toward them.

At the same time, Brooke walked up. She had a

162

towel around her and she stood next to Kari.

Lilly was out of breath when she came up beside Braden. "Goodbyes are sad." She hugged Brooke and then Kari. "Thanks for hanging out with us."

"It was fun." Brooke stepped back beside Kari.

They stood there in silence, all four of them. "It's weird." Braden shrugged. "We might never see each other again."

He was right. Kari felt a little sick to her stomach because the goodbyes were coming. Now, and at the end of the school year. So many goodbyes. And there was nothing they could do about them.

Braden pulled something from his pocket. "Here . . ." He held up a sand dollar and gave it to Kari. "I found this on the beach earlier. It's for you." He smiled. "So you can remember us when you get back to Michigan."

A sand dollar.

Kari couldn't believe it. She ran her thumb over the surface of the shell and looked at Braden again. "Thanks." Their eyes held for a few seconds. "I won't forget you." She turned to Lilly. "You, either."

Lilly and Brooke were quiet. Like none of them wanted the moment to end.

"Braden, Lilly." His dad called loud from the back of the house. "Let's go."

"It's time." Braden rocked back and forth on his toes. He took a step toward Kari and hugged her. Super quick. "Have fun in Indiana. And sorry for crashing into you on that first day."

Kari laughed at the memory. "See you, Braden."

"See you later." He gave her and Brooke a last smile and then jogged up the hill. Lilly said goodbye to both of them, too, and did the same. And that was that.

Spring break was over.

But as Kari and her family loaded up the car and headed back to Ann Arbor, she knew one thing for sure. If she could make such good friends in one week, then she could make new friends anywhere.

Even in a place like Bloomington, Indiana.

14

Samson the Butterfly

ASHLEY

Finally it was spring in Ann Arbor, and this week Ashley's class was hatching eight cocoons, which were set up in an aquarium with twigs and leaves and rocks. Every day they checked on them to see if they were about to become butterflies.

Ashley could see the cocoons very well because they sat on the windowsill, closest to her desk. Which was why she was having the most difficult time actually listening to Miss Wilson.

Her teacher was talking about a new spelling word. *Pervasive.* That was the word today. Miss Wilson wanted all of them to practice using it in a sentence at home. Or maybe it was a different word. Ashley wasn't totally sure.

Because . . . the cocoons.

Ashley put her chin in her hands and stared at the aquarium where they were. It must be so tight in those cocoons. What would a caterpillar be thinking all smashed in such a small space and not able to—

All the sudden one of the cocoons moved. Ashley jumped to her feet. "Miss Wilson!" She waved both hands over her head, her eyes fixed on the cocoon. "It's moving! One of them is moving."

With this, Ashley's whole class, including Miss Wilson, ran over to watch. Ashley had a front-row seat, which was the best part of the moment. She saved a spot for Lydia right next to her.

"Wow." Lydia pressed her face close to the glass. "I think you're right. It's moving."

"It's not moving, Baxter." Eric Powers was right behind them. He laughed. "You're seeing things."

Ashley turned around very slowly, so Eric would know that he was not making her happy. "It's Ashley." She lowered her chin and stared straight at him. "Not Baxter. And you're on thin ice here."

"Thin ice?" Eric laughed, and his three friends on either side of him did the same thing. "Okay, Baxter." He laughed once more. "Whatever you say. The cocoon isn't moving."

"Actually"—Miss Wilson took a close look through the screen at the top of the aquarium—"I think it might be. Just a little." The teacher stood straighter. "But we still have a long time before we'll see any butterflies. Maybe by tomorrow."

Miss Wilson was right. The next day when they came in from lunch four beautiful butterflies had hatched from four cocoons! They were yellow with blue lines and black dots.

The class circled around the glass container. They were the most amazing creations Ashley had ever seen. For sure God was the best artist of all time. How could they go from slow crawly little caterpillars to these beautiful flying pieces of art?

"Boys and girls . . ." Miss Wilson joined the group near the aquarium. "You know what's next. It's time to release them."

"Oh, no." Ashley's shoulders fell. Not so soon! "Oh no, oh no."

"What?" Lydia looked at her.

"My sadness is pervasive." There. Ashley had used the new word. But it didn't make her feel any better. She leaned against Lydia and dropped her head in her hands for a few seconds. "Don't you wish we could keep them forever?"

"No." Lydia pushed Ashley back up so she wouldn't fall. "You're being a little dramatic."

Ashley couldn't believe it. "Why don't you want to keep them?"

"Because." Lydia shook her head. "They'll die if they don't get set free!"

True. Ashley hadn't thought of that. She just hated that they were going to be gone. "They grow up so fast."

This time Lydia laughed out loud. "You really are the funniest person I know, Ashley Baxter."

Miss Wilson carried the aquarium as she led the class outside. Everyone gathered around her. Ashley held her breath, her face close to the glass. "Goodbye, little butterflies," she whispered.

Everyone was talking at once, so Miss Wilson had to talk loud. "Quiet down. Listen up, boys and girls." She put her hand over the top of the butterfly enclosure. "We raised them and saw them hatch. Now let's watch them fly!"

And just like that she opened the top and—one by one—the butterflies moved their wings and lifted into the air, making their way free of the aquarium.

Into the wild.

They fluttered through the warm spring day and took different directions. One flew toward the closest tree. Two moved low along the grass. The last one flew straight up until he was near the roof of the school.

For once in her life, Ashley was speechless.

"All right"—Miss Wilson clapped—"back to the classroom. We've got a test to prepare for!" The boys and girls groaned as she hurried them all back inside.

Ashley felt a tap at her side and she turned to see Eric. Her least favorite person. "Hey, Baxter. Wanna race to the door?"

"Please." Ashley rolled her eyes. "You know you'll lose, Eric!" She nudged him back. "And don't call me Baxter!"

"Whatever." He locked his eyes on hers. "Come on! Three . . . two . . . one . . ."

"Go!" Ashley took off, and beside her so did Eric.

At first she had a head start, but then he caught up and started moving ahead. Two steps, four steps, six steps ahead of her. Suddenly the door was in front of them and Ashley pushed herself as hard as she could.

But it wasn't enough.

Eric slapped the door first.

"Ha! I win!" He looked like a rooster with his chest all puffed out.

"Who cares?" Ashley made a face at him. "I'll get you next time."

The final few hours of the day dragged by. Grammar this. English that. If only she cared about all this school stuff the way Brooke and Kari and Erin did. All Ashley wanted to do was bring her journal to school and draw.

Then right in the middle of multiplication it happened. A beautiful blue and yellow butterfly danced up close to the window. Almost as if the butterfly wanted to tell Ashley hello. This butterfly looked like a boy, so right there in her own heart Ashley named him Samson.

He looked so happy. Ashley hoped Samson stayed that way forever. "Hello, Samson," Ashley whispered.

Lydia turned and stared at her. "Who's Samson?" She talked soft so Miss Wilson wouldn't hear.

"My butterfly." Ashley pointed to the window. "I named him Samson."

For a few more seconds Lydia stared at her. Then she shook her head and looked back at Miss Wilson.

Ashley could still see the butterfly hanging around near the window. Which may not have been the smartest choice. Some kid on the playground might catch him. "Samson," she whispered again, this time with more enthusiasm. "Fly! Be free!"

And he did.

He flew off to the sky toward other adventures. And Ashley spent the rest of the day wishing she could go with him.

15

A Trillion Pink Flowers

ASHLEY

Ashley was mad at herself.

She didn't pay attention in class, and now she had extra homework. Miss Wilson always said what you didn't get done in class, you had to do later. So now it was after school and Ashley was sprawled out on her bed, in her room, on this warm spring day working on math.

Her workbook was open to the right page. Ashley stared at all the little numbers. And the problems stared right straight back at her. Ashley tapped her pencil on the page. If only Miss Wilson didn't make them do so many problems.

Something caught her attention outside. Flowers! How come she hadn't noticed this? The beautiful tree right outside her bedroom window had decided it was spring and now it was full of a trillion pink flowers! "Hello, flowers!" Ashley jumped up and went to the window. "Hello, tree! Hello, blossoms! Happy spring to all of you!"

She put her hand against the glass. That's when she saw the giant red and white FOR SALE sign at the end of their driveway. Her stomach started to sink, the way it did every time she noticed that thing. *Don't think about it, Ashley,* she told herself. *Look at the flowers.*

That's right. She shifted so she could only see the tree in front of the window. The bunches of flowers looked like the most amazing pink clouds, hanging on the branches just for her. Like something from a dream, a beautiful sight she could sketch in her special journal and—

Ashley turned fast and looked at her math book on the bed.

Math! What was she doing? She had to get her work done. A sigh came from inside her. This was the last spring she would ever see the pink flowers outside her window here at this house. Next spring they'd live in Bloomington. And there was no telling if Bloomington even had flowers.

Or maybe it would have different flowers. Blooming flowers. Who could tell?

Which was why it really was too bad she had math on a day like this.

Ashley picked up her pencil and tapped the open book again. Problem 1 wasn't too hard. Fifteen times four equals . . . Sixty. Yes, she could do this. She wrote the answer in the space.

But at the same time she had an idea.

Maybe she could do a quick sketch of the pretty flowers and the tree and then she would have a clear head to do math. Yes! That was a great idea.

Of course, Mom did say she was supposed to do her math first. Hmm . . . She chewed on her pencil. Thinking. She liked how the teeth marks looked in the yellow painted wood.

What could it hurt? She wouldn't spend too much time on the drawing. She hopped off her bed and grabbed her journal from the top of the dresser. Just a quick sketch. She'd get back to her homework in no time.

However, the second she looked out the window, Ashley had another idea. The drawing would be so much better if she went outside! Under the tree. Her dad had put a nice bench there last spring, so that would be the perfect place.

She took her journal and a pencil and with quiet feet she tiptoed down the stairs. Erin and Brooke were at the kitchen counter doing homework. Kari was cutting up an apple, and Luke and Mom were apparently in the backyard shooting baskets.

That's all Luke wanted to do anymore, play basketball.

Which was perfect in this exact minute, because the pink-flowered tree was out front. Ashley snuck through the front door and ran to the tree.

She would just do a quick sketch and then run back upstairs.

Still moving as quiet as she could she took her seat beneath the tree. The view was perfect. Plus she felt like James Bond on a secret mission. Actually Jane Bond. Yes, that was it. She was *Jane* Bond!

Her breathing was faster than usual from all the excitement.

Never mind that, she told herself. *Focus on the tree.* Which was just what she did. For a long time. First the tree, then she began to sketch the pink blossoms. So much beauty and color tucked inside a little teeny, tiny pod. Like a sleeping bag. She made half-circular motions as leaves. And she shaded them in. Next she made small lines on the leaves.

Who needs math when you could do this?

Right in that instant a dark shadow fell over her journal page. "Hey." She didn't look up. "You're blocking my . . ." Ashley looked up and her breath stopped. "Mom."

Her mom raised her eyebrows, but she didn't say anything. So Ashley tried to fill the space. Her words came in a hurry.

"Hello, beautiful mother." Ashley swallowed. "I must say . . . you look just . . . perfectly lovely today. And this weather . . . wow." Ashley smiled and blinked a few times. Maybe her mom had forgotten about the math. *Please, God, let her forget about the math.*

"Ashley." A loud breath came from between her mother's lips. "What in the world are you doing out here?"

"Me?" Ashley put her hand over her chest. She looked up at the flowers and then back at her mother. "I'm being a nature lover, Mom." She pointed up. "Have you seen those blossoms? They're the brightest pink."

"You're supposed to be doing your math." She held out her hand. "Give me your journal."

Ashley held her journal close to her heart. The pink blossoms were just coming to life. "I don't think I can do that. Plus I'm very sorry." She hoped her mother could see she was telling the truth. "Please, can I keep it?"

"Give me your book." Mom wasn't budging. Not today.

"I will ask just one thing of you, Mother." Ashley handed the journal over. "Take good care of it."

"And *I* will ask just one thing, Ashley." Her

mother looked extra-serious. "Do your math. Now." She didn't yell, but she did point to the front door. "Upstairs."

"Yes, ma'am." It was time to get moving. Ashley hurried ahead of her mom. Who cared about math, anyway? When would she ever need to know how to multiply? She just wanted to draw.

But she would do the work and she would do it now. So she could get her journal back and do something that mattered to her. Ashley pressed her teeth together. Her determination never felt so strong.

Back in her room, she took her workbook to the desk she shared with Kari and she sat down. The math problems stared at her again. "I'll take care of you," she told them. "Every single one of you."

The first problem had an eight in it. And eights are a lot like flowers. So even though she tried everything inside her to get the math problems finished, an hour later the page was covered with the prettiest blossoms.

Just like on the tree outside her window.

Suddenly there was a sound outside her door.

She looked at her math book and gasped. What had she done? She slammed the book shut and turned toward the door just as her mom opened it.

"Time for dinner." Her mother smiled like she trusted Ashley completely. "Did you finish?"

"Yes. Every one." The words jumped out of her mouth before she could catch them. Even though they weren't true.

"Okay, then. Good girl." Mom's eyes were sweet and happy. "Getting your work done is the right thing to do."

"Yes." Ashley gulped. "Yes, Mom."

"You can have your journal back after we eat." She stopped. "You should try writing in it sometime. That's what it's supposed to be for."

When she was gone, Ashley's heart beat hard in her throat. That's what Kari had said. The journal was for writing. But maybe Ashley wasn't a writer. Maybe she liked drawing better. The walls felt like they were moving in toward her, and even the blossoms on the tree seemed to laugh at her.

What was going to happen to her? She had filled her entire math assignment with flowers.

And somehow her mom had forgotten to check her work. Which meant Ashley hadn't only sketched flower blossoms where her math work was supposed to go. She had done the unthinkable.

She had lied to her very own mother.

16

The Big Lie

ASHLEY

The lie was growing.

Through dinner it felt like a bag of potatoes on Ashley's shoulders and it got heavier later on when her mom gave Ashley her journal back. By the time Ashley went to bed it felt like two sacks of potatoes.

Because lies are hard to carry. They get heavier all the time.

Ashley should've known that.

The next day at school her steps were slower than usual. Especially because after lunch Miss Wilson would ask for the math workbooks from kids who hadn't finished the problems in class and then . . .

Well, that would be the end of everything.

At their lunch table, Lydia had no trouble eating her grilled cheese sandwich and sliced orange. But Ashley couldn't eat a single bite. She tried and it tasted like wet cardboard.

It took Lydia a few minutes to notice. "You're not eating."

Ashley shook her head. "I drew blossoms."

Lydia scrunched her face into a wrinkle. "What?"

"I drew blossoms." Ashley stared straight down at her cold grilled cheese sandwich. She was the worst student in fourth grade. All of fourth grade. Everywhere in the world.

"Ashley." Lydia leaned closer. "Look at me."

In slow motion, Ashley lifted her eyes and looked at her friend. "Yes?"

"What blossoms?" Lydia took another bite of her sandwich. She looked confused.

"Instead of doing the math problems." Ashley breathed out. Her shoulders sank some. "I drew flower blossoms where the answers were supposed to be."

Lydia's eyes got big. "Oh, no!" She sat up

straight again, but her eyes never left Ashley's. "You're gonna be in big trouble."

"Yes." Ashley pushed her plate away. The smell of cold fried cheese wasn't helping. "Also I lied about it . . . to my mom."

Somehow Lydia's eyes got even bigger. This time she didn't say anything. She just kept eating her sandwich and watching Ashley. Every now and then she would shake her head. When lunch was over she patted Ashley's hand. "I'll still be your friend. No matter what happens."

"Thank you."

Ashley felt sick on the way back to the classroom and even sicker when Miss Wilson came to collect her math book. "Ashley. Your homework?" She waited.

The lie had to stop somewhere. Ashley handed over her book. "I didn't do it." A thought hit at just that instant. "But you love art, right, Miss Wilson?"

"Art?"

"Because." Ashley tried to smile. "Where the answers should be there is a lovely sketch of some tree blossoms from just outside my window."

"What?" Miss Wilson stood there. She opened Ashley's workbook and stared at the drawing. Her eyes got darker than before. "Ashley. I'm very disappointed." She held the book so Ashley could see it. Then she tapped hard on the beautiful blossoms. "This is not an option."

Ashley decided to be honest again. "I think the problem is that deep in my heart I don't like math." Ashley gave Miss Wilson a little smile. "I'm not good at it. So I drew blossoms."

Next to her Lydia looked down at her desk, and shook her head. A few seats back Ashley saw Eric Powers lean closer, like he was trying to hear what was happening.

The whole class was starting to notice.

"You will be marked down for this, Ashley." Miss Wilson gave her a last sad look. She handed the workbook back to Ashley. "And you'll have to do the work on a clean sheet of paper tonight. Math is not optional."

Just like Lydia had said, Ashley was in trouble. Big trouble.

Ashley sat still, not blinking. Her face felt hot

and sweaty. What would her parents say when they found out? She waited until Miss Wilson was facing the blackboard. Then she leaned close to Lydia and whispered very soft. "Hey."

Lydia shook her head, like this was not the time.

"Do you think I could live with you?"

"No." Her friend scrunched up her face again. "Your family would miss you too much."

Ashley sat back in her seat. Well, that was it. She was out of options. Then a possibility filled her mind. Her parents loved her, right? They would not send her to jail for this crime. Plus the sack of potatoes was getting too heavy to carry. Which left her with just one choice.

She would go home after school and tell her mom the truth.

Ashley couldn't believe the news.

She had planned the perfect time to tell her parents about the Big Lie and to get to work on her math problems. That time was going to be long after dinner. So Ashley could have a nice afternoon and evening playing outside first.

But something terrible had happened.

Miss Wilson had called her mother even before Ashley got home from school. Before her dad came home from work early like he always did on Wednesdays. With no warning at all, Miss Wilson had called and told them the news. And then her mom had brought Ashley inside before even a single hour of fun. While all the other kids kept playing.

"Come to the dining room," her dad told her. His voice was frustrated.

Ashley felt like she was walking the plank. She could feel the shaky wood beneath her nervous feet. She would walk to the edge and sink to the bottom of the ocean. She could already feel the cold water.

But instead, she was in the dry dining room. She sat across from her parents and blinked a few times.

"Let me see if I have this right." Dad looked hard at her. "You drew a picture instead of doing your math." He put his elbows on the table and leaned closer. "And then you lied to your mother about it?"

Ashley struggled for any possible explanation. "Technically it wasn't a picture." She started to smile and then changed her mind. "It was flower blossoms."

"Ashley." He didn't yell. But his voice was angry. "Please answer the question."

Tell the truth, she told herself. *You have to tell the truth.* She squeezed her eyes shut and let her answer come. "Yes!" She covered her face with her hands. "I drew blossoms instead of answers and then I lied about it."

"Look at us." Her mom sounded extra-serious.

Ashley lowered her hands a few inches and turned to her mother. She was sitting right next to her dad. They were like a jury all lined up. A sad feeling came over Ashley and tears gathered in her eyes. "I'm sorry."

"I hope so." Dad leaned back in his chair and folded his arms. "We expect more from you, Ashley. A lot more."

A single tear fell onto her cheek. "Maybe you shouldn't expect so much."

Just then Brooke came down the stairs. She was happy and lighthearted as usual. She had her Bible under her arm. Brooke was the picture of every-thing perfect.

Ashley watched her parents' faces. "Hello, dear." Their dad's voice was much kinder. He stood and hugged Brooke. "You're headed to youth group?"

"Yes." Brooke smiled. "Jenny's mother is picking me up!"

Now their mother was on her feet, too. And she was also hugging Brooke. Like she was going away for the summer and not just for the night. "Homework done?"

"Of course." Brooke looked as happy as a kid with cake.

There was a honking sound outside and Brooke waved. "See you later!" She smiled at Ashley. "See ya, Ashley."

"See ya." Ashley looked down at her hands. She felt worse. She'd never make her parents this happy.

Brooke grinned at their mom and dad. "Love you!"

"Love you, too." They both said it at once. They might as well have said they loved Brooke the most. Because that much was obvious.

When the door shut behind Brooke, Ashley looked at her parents. Silence. They returned to their seats at the table. "What do you have to say for yourself?" Trouble took over Mom's face again. "I can't believe you'd lie to me."

"Okay." Ashley swallowed hard.

"Okay what?" Her mom's voice was higher than before.

Ashley thought fast. "Okay, maybe it's better if you don't believe it." Another tiny smile. "Then we could pretend it never happened."

"We won't pretend anything of that sort." Her dad took a long breath. "Ashley, you are a Baxter. Remember what we say about lies?"

Ever since the lie, Ashley had tried to forget. But the truth was there. She nodded. "You don't love someone you lie to . . . and you don't lie to someone you love."

"Yes." For the first time since they sat down, Dad looked a little less upset. "Baxters don't lie. We face the truth. Even if it means getting in trouble."

Ashley pictured herself at a cold desk in a boarding school. Her parents would probably send her off and the place would be run by a mean headmistress and Ashley would have to scrub floors like in *Little Orphan Annie*. For the rest of her life.

"You'll go straight to your room when we're done, and finish your math. However long it takes." Their dad looked at Mom. "Elizabeth, I have work to do tonight. Maybe you could help her."

"I will." Her mom looked tired. "Ashley, homework is serious business. Math, too. These things are not optional."

They were the same words Miss Wilson had used. Ashley nodded. "Yes, ma'am."

"You need to be a better student." Her dad looked at her for a long minute. "The kind of student Brooke is. Maybe you could learn from her."

Brooke? Ashley felt her throat get tight. "But . . . Brooke doesn't even like to draw."

"Drawing is secondary." Her mom sounded frustrated again. "You have to do what matters, Ashley."

What matters? Ashley felt sick again. Drawing didn't matter? Be like Brooke? She thought about Brooke and how she spent her time: reading, studying, speech and debate? Quiet and serious all the time? Ashley couldn't think of a worse punishment. She felt the tears coming again.

"Don't be upset." Her dad stood and came to her. "Stand up."

Ashley obeyed. What choice did she have?

Dad hugged her and took gentle hold of her chin. His eyes were softer now. "Get your work done. Now." He smiled. "I know you can do it."

His words stayed inside her as she walked up to her room and started untangling the math problems. Every so often an angry tear would fall on the clean sheet of paper. But Ashley didn't care. She had bigger problems.

No more drawing.

No more dreaming.

As she worked on her homework, she felt herself getting stronger. She decided that if her parents wanted her to be more serious about school, then that's exactly what she would do. Find a way to be more serious. More hours for homework. Better grades. And by the end of the night she was ready to do the one thing her parents wanted most of all.

She was ready to be more like Brooke.

17

The New Coach

ASHLEY

Math was like a mountain Ashley could never climb. No matter how hard she tried to be like Brooke, there was one missing piece.

Ashley hated math. Brooke loved it.

So how could she ever actually be like Brooke?

That Saturday, though, math and numbers and common denominators didn't matter at all. Because today was something more wonderful than spring.

Soccer!

Drawing was Ashley's first best talent, but soccer was a close second. That's what her dad always said. A very close second. Ashley was a forward, which meant she was at the front of the field. The place where all the scoring happened. Ashley's foot was more like a boot.

That's what Ashley's teammates always said. "You've got a good boot, Ash!"

They didn't actually mean a boot, of course. You couldn't play soccer in boots. It meant that Ashley kicked hard and lots of times she sent the ball straight into the goal.

Ashley could hardly wait for practice. Finally, something other than math.

As soon as she and Kari walked onto the soccer field, Ashley noticed something wonderful. Their team had a new coach! Last year's coach had been a large, loud man who smelled like hot dogs. A yeller, Kari's dad called him. Almost every game last year one of the girls on the team would cry.

Which almost ruined soccer for everyone. Even Ashley.

The coach this year looked like a soccer player. She was tall with a ponytail and she wore a pink baseball cap. She had a sweet smile. And she looked like someone Kari would want to be her coach.

As soon as Ashley saw her, she started to run.

"Come on." She reached out for Kari's hand. "Let's sign in!"

But Kari stopped and shook her head. "I'm not sure. I heard something terrible."

"Huh?" Ashley put on the brakes. She turned to her sister. "What do you mean? What's terrible?" She looked back at the sign-in area. "We have a new coach."

"I see that." Kari crossed her arms.

Ashley tried to understand. "What did you hear?"

"I don't want to talk about it. Brittany told me at school yesterday." Kari moved her toe around in the grass. "I just remembered when Dad dropped us off."

Kari's words weren't lining up. "What did Brittany tell you?"

"Nothing." Kari waved her hand around. She acted like they'd already lost their first game. Finally Kari looked up. "It's just . . . what if I'm not good enough?"

"You?" Ashley couldn't make sense of her sister's statement. "Don't be silly. You're already on

the team. Plus, Brittany doesn't even play soccer."
Ashley wanted to get going. "Come on!"

"You go." Kari bit her lip. She set her gear bag on
the grass in front of her. "I need to change shoes."

Ashley looked at her sister's tennis shoes. She
had a point. Cleats were required here.

"Girls!" They both turned to see their dad
standing near their family van. Dad usually stayed
for practice, but he told them he had to spend a
few hours at the hospital working this morning. He
smiled at them. "Have fun!"

They smiled and waved at him. But Kari's smile
didn't last long.

Ashley had a thought. "Want me to wait? While
you put on your cleats?"

"That's okay." Kari's expression looked nervous.
Like a kindergarten kid on the first day of school.
She shook her head. "I'll catch up."

Ashley wasn't so sure. She'd never seen Kari act
like this. No, her sister wasn't the best player on
the team. But she was a good midfielder. She was
always running around, kicking the ball to someone who could actually score.

Like Ashley.

"All right." Ashley gave her sister a quick smile. "See you in a bit."

She ran toward the coach and excitement filled her to overflowing. All around her the girls seemed to feel the same way. A few were kicking a ball. Some dribbled around orange cones for practice.

Ashley recognized most of the girls from school, but a few were new. Lydia came running up beside her. "I just got here." She sounded out of breath from happiness. Lydia had a boot, too. "Can you believe it? Soccer season!"

"Finally!" Ashley hugged her friend. They walked together to the new coach. The woman had a clipboard and a bag of soccer balls. After they signed in, the coach used a whistle to get the girls' attention.

"Everyone come sit down." Her voice was loud, but there was a smile tucked inside it. "Welcome to soccer."

Ashley looked over her shoulder. Kari was just walking up, slower than the other girls. "Over here." Ashley said the words but she kept the sound out.

She patted on the grass next to her and Lydia.

Kari came and sat down, but she looked sick.

"You okay?"

"I'm fine."

"Girls." The coach still looked happy. Ashley wanted to keep it that way. The coach looked straight at them. "Please pay attention."

Ashley nodded. Lydia and Kari did the same thing. Poor Lydia. She was always getting in trouble just for sitting next to Ashley. In class and now here. Ashley patted her friend on the back. "Sorry, Lydia."

Her friend didn't look at her. "Shhh."

"Right. Quiet." Ashley nodded and looked at the front of the group of girls.

The coach was waiting.

When Ashley stopped talking the woman raised her voice. "Okay, good morning, girls. I'm Coach Kelly." She looked around at the group. "Let's figure out our team name first." She looked around. "Anyone have a suggestion?"

Ashley stood straight up. "Me!" She'd been thinking about this since last year. They were the

Little Kickers last year. Now that seemed like a baby name.

"You can sit down, Ashley." Coach Kelly did a short laugh. "Okay, what's your idea?"

"The Mighty Dolphins." Ashley couldn't actually sit back down. Not yet. She put her hands together out in front of her and wove around in little half circles for a minute. "See? A dolphin has a strong tail. He can move in and out of other fish in a flash. Also . . ." She stopped weaving and looked at Kari and Lydia and the other girls, and finally back at Coach Kelly. "Who wouldn't want to be a Mighty Dolphin?"

The coach blinked a few times. "Okay." She looked at the group. "Anyone else?"

No one had a better suggestion. No one had any suggestions. Ashley felt excited but tried not to let it show. Mighty Dolphins was her favorite team name ever.

"Okay, then." Coach laughed again. "We are the Mighty Dolphins." She looked at her clipboard. As she did her smile collapsed. "Now, please sit down, Ashley."

"Yes, ma'am." Ashley sat.

"One thing before we get started." Coach Kelly's tone seemed sort of unhappy.

Ashley's heart started to run faster inside her.

The coach looked around again. "I'm afraid I have some tough news today."

Ashley pulled her knees to her chest. What was this? The coach was afraid of some bad news? What could be so bad? They hadn't even started. Ashley listened.

"So here's the situation." Coach Kelly raised her cap a bit. "Too many girls came out for soccer." She waited. "We're going to pick some of you today for the Mighty Dolphins. The rest of you will play on a different team." She smiled like that was a good thing. "Everyone will get to play. Just not on this team. This will be a Three-A team. The other one will play a division down, at Two A."

Ashley felt a tap on her shoulder. She turned, and Kari gave her a little nod. "See?" she whispered. "Brittany knew."

Ashley let the truth sink in. She wasn't worried about making the team. But what about her sister?

Soccer wasn't Kari's best talent. No wonder she was worried. Ashley stared at the grass.

Coach Kelly explained that first they were going to do a passing drill. That sounded easy enough. But then Ashley looked at Kari. Her sister's eyes were filling up. Ashley put her arm around Kari's shoulders. "It's okay. You're good at passing."

"I don't know." Kari stood, and Ashley and Lydia joined her. The three of them took their places on the field. Then Coach Kelly blew her whistle.

And with that the season started!

Ashley got the ball from Lydia. She dribbled a few feet and kicked the ball to Kari. It was a perfect pass, but Kari was out of position, playing more in the backfield. She must've been nervous, because the ball went zooming past her.

Everyone stopped while Kari ran after the ball. Ashley shared a look with Lydia. Anyone could make a mistake, but if Kari played like this, she was in big trouble. Ashley and Lydia both knew it.

The coach blew her whistle. "Kari. You're supposed to be in the middle. That means try to be ready for every pass."

Ashley watched Kari move to midfield. She walked like her feet weighed a hundred pounds. Lydia kicked the ball into action again. They were six passes into the drill when Kari got the ball.

"I'm open!" Ashley yelled.

But this seemed to make Kari even more nervous. Instead of passing, she took the ball by herself to the goal.

Most of the girls stopped and watched.

Coach Kelly blew the whistle again. "Kari Baxter. You understand the drill, right? You have to pass. Your sister was open." She looked at the other players. "Share the ball, girls. That's what soccer is about."

Ashley saw Kari dab at her eyes. *Poor Kari*, Ashley thought. This just wasn't her day. If she kept this up she wouldn't get a spot on the team.

And that would be the worst possible news ever.

18

The Almost Mighty Dolphins

ASHLEY

Coach Kelly announced it was time for shooting drills and Ashley raised both hands in the air. "Yes!" She patted Lydia and Kari on their backs. "Finally some action out here!"

The best part of soccer was shooting the ball. Ashley loved this part. But as they ran to their places, Ashley noticed that Kari looked even more upset than before.

"You okay?" Ashley moved closer to her sister.

"Not really." Kari put her hands on her hips. "I meant to pass the ball to you. I'm sorry, Ash. I . . . I just panicked."

"It was an honest mistake." Ashley put her arm

around Kari's shoulders. "Remember what Dad says when we mess up?"

"What?" Kari took a long breath. Like maybe she was feeling a little better.

"He says move on. So let's do that." Ashley clapped her hands a few times. "You're a good player. You got this."

The drill was simple. Half the team was on offense, half on defense. The offense needed to make five passes and then whoever had the ball was supposed to shoot. Kari was on the team with Ashley and Lydia.

Ashley had the ball first. She passed it to Lydia, who passed it across the field to Kari. Kari dodged two defenders and passed it back to Lydia. So far so good.

They were near the goal and they'd done five passes. Lydia passed the ball to Ashley and she could see the goal. Feel it. This would be her first score of the season. She needed this one.

But at the same time Ashley spotted Kari open on the other side of the field.

And right in that moment, Ashley knew. Kari needed the goal more. She passed the ball to her sister and *boom!*

Kari scored!

Ashley ran to her sister and the two hugged and high-fived. Lydia and the other girls on their team joined them.

"Why'd you do that?" Kari looked at her. Her face said she couldn't believe the goal had actually happened.

"You were open." Ashley grinned. "The open player gets the worm."

Kari laughed, and like that the afternoon was better. It was the turnaround Kari seemed to need. The rest of practice she didn't miss a single ball and her passes were almost perfect. And even though she didn't score again, Ashley really thought Kari was good enough to make the team.

She had to be.

Two hours flew by and Ashley was dripping with sweat by the time they circled up. Coach Kelly had her clipboard again and rallied the girls one last time for the day. "Okay." She looked at everyone.

"You were all very good. I'd love to have any of you on my team."

Here we go, Ashley thought. She looked at Kari sitting beside her. Lydia seemed to do the same thing. They were all a little worried.

Coach Kelly started reading off names. "Ashley Baxter. Lydia Green." The list seemed very long. Only not one name was Kari's.

Kari seemed to shrivel up, like she was shrinking a bit more with every name the coach said. And then the woman took a big breath. "That's it. If I didn't read your name, you'll be getting a call from Coach Brown in the Two-A Division. He'll tell you when your practices start."

Her words blended together and landed like rain over Ashley. What had just happened? Kari wasn't on the team? Ashley stared at the grass and then real fast she looked at Kari.

Tears were swimming down her sister's face.

"Oh, Kari." Lydia put her hand on Kari's shoulder. "There must be a mistake. You played great today."

Ashley couldn't believe it. She looked from Kari

to the front of the group of girls. Only five players hadn't made the team. None of them were crying. They were laughing and playing tag. Like they didn't care what team they played on.

But it actually mattered to Kari.

Ashley had something to say about this. Without checking with Lydia or Kari, Ashley stood and walked up to Coach Kelly. "Excuse me."

The coach looked at her. "Ashley!" She smiled. "Congratulations! You played very well today. You definitely have a boot."

"Yes, well. Thank you." She lifted her chin. Someone had to fight for Kari. "But I have a question. Or a situation . . ."

"Okay . . ." Coach Kelly set the bag of soccer balls down. The sun was hot on their shoulders now, and the coach looked ready to leave.

"It's about my sister." Ashley stood as tall as she could. "I think Kari should be on our team. She played very good." Ashley gave the coach a curious look. "Could you give her another chance?"

For a few seconds Coach Kelly said nothing. Then she nodded slow and sure. "I'll think about that." She patted Ashley's shoulder. "For now, though, she's on the other team."

Before Ashley could say anything else, the coach picked up the bag of balls and walked toward the parking lot.

By then Ashley's dad was coming across the field to get them. His smile looked full of hope. He clearly had no idea what had just happened. But right then he looked at Kari and his smile melted away in the hot afternoon.

He could clearly tell she was upset.

Ashley walked back to Kari just as their dad reached them both. Kari wasn't crying as hard now. Ashley understood. Her sister was trying to be brave.

"What happened?" Their dad looked from Kari to Ashley.

"Let's talk about it in the car." Ashley took her father's hand. "Okay?"

"Sure." Their dad looked at Kari. "Honey . . . are you okay?"

"Dad." Ashley put her finger to her lips. "In the car. Please."

On the drive home Kari explained what had happened. She had more tears as she talked about it. Ashley felt so sorry for her sister, she hoped the coach would change her mind and let Kari be a Mighty Dolphin. The whole thing seemed so unfair. "You had the best goal of the day." Ashley sat in the backseat so Kari could be up front with Dad.

"Yeah. Because of you." Kari glanced back at her. She sounded thankful and frustrated at the same time. She did a loud outbreath. "I don't know what happened. I used to be really good."

Their dad reached for Kari's hand. "I'm so sorry." Ashley watched him wrap his fingers around Kari's, the way he used to do when the girls were little. "I wish I could make things better. But I can tell you this . . ." He turned nice eyes to Kari. "God has good plans for you. That's a promise from the Bible. Even if His plans might not be for you to play on this soccer team."

They came in the house like a black rain cloud. Right away Mom met them near the door with curious eyes. "What happened?"

Between Ashley and Kari, the story spilled out. Their mom asked Kari to help her in the kitchen. So they could talk. That's when Ashley realized how sad she felt. Kari had always been on her soccer team. Ever since they were five and six.

Without Kari they wouldn't be the same team. They'd have to change their name, even. The Mighty Dolphins was a name that meant Kari was on the team. Kari helped make them mighty. Now they would have to be something else.

The Almost Mighty Dolphins.

19

The Awful Tower

ASHLEY

Saturday was fading. Brooke and Erin and Luke were playing basketball in the driveway, so Dad went outside to join them.

Ashley looked around. She spotted her journal on the kitchen counter. It was the perfect something to get her mind off the trouble of the day. She grabbed a pencil and the book and found a seat on the sofa, right near the window. Her view also included Mom and Kari.

Ashley liked knowing they were nearby.

She stared at a blank page and a whole lot of dreams danced through her mind. A mountain? No, she had drawn that a week ago. A birthday cake? No, too easy. Then she had an idea.

"Paris!" She couldn't stop the word from slipping out.

From the kitchen, her mom looked her way. "What?"

"Nothing." Ashley smiled. She really had to work on her words just jumping ahead of her. She waved to her mom. "I'm fine."

She turned her attention back to the empty page. Yes, Paris was perfect. Lydia had gone last spring and just Friday she had brought her photo album to class for show-and-tell.

Ashley couldn't believe the flowers and the river and the buildings. But most of all she was amazed at the Awful Tower. She remembered seeing it in a movie and also on the key chain Lydia had bought her.

She drew some grass, little tiny lines in different directions. Because like people, grass didn't grow straight and perfect every time. Then she sketched trees. Five skinny trunks with big tops, lots of leaves and springtime flowers.

Last she worked on the Awful Tower. Two lines starting a ways apart and meeting up in the middle.

Ashley was just about to start filling in the tower beams when Brooke came inside. She was breathing hard from basketball. She looked at Ashley. "Doing your math?"

For a quick moment Ashley didn't know what to say.

Their mom looked at Ashley. "That's a good question. Is your homework done, Ash?"

Ashley stared at Brooke. Why did she have to ruin a perfectly good drawing hour? She cleared her throat and tried to look proper. "I plan to do my homework after dinner." She gave a single nod. "Because good nutrition is a part of any successful homework plan."

"Ashley." Her mom made a serious face. "You know our deal."

The deal was that Ashley didn't get punished for lying the other day, so long as she did her homework first before drawing or playing . . . the rest of the school year. Ashley tapped her pencil on the page. She was so close to finishing.

"Ashley?" Mom was waiting.

"Okay." Ashley shot Brooke a mean look. "I'll get right to it."

Kari sent Ashley a sad look. Yes, Kari understood.

Ashley turned to Brooke. If her oldest sister could tell Ashley was frustrated with her, she didn't act like it. Instead she walked into the living room right up to Ashley. "You're drawing again?"

"Brooke, you know I like drawing. I draw every day."

"Sure. Making pictures is fun." Brooke gave her a sympathy smile. "Just don't let a hobby distract you from the important things." Brooke looked back at their mother. "Right, Mom?"

"Right." Their mom was making bean soup. Ashley's absolute worst dinner. "You need to focus on your studies, Ashley."

Again Kari sent a look at Ashley that said she would do something to help if she could.

All motherly, Brooke nodded. "Without good grades, you'll never get into college." She smiled again. "You need to think about that, Ashley."

What Ashley didn't need at this very moment was two moms. Now she felt trapped. "College?" Ashley looked at her drawing and then past Brooke to their mom. "Someone give me a break. I'm only ten years old. College is a hundred years away."

"But you're behind," Brooke added. She seemed concerned but Ashley knew better. Her sister was causing trouble just because that's what thirteen-year-old sisters sometimes do. Ashley pressed her lips together and stared at Brooke. "You may think I'm behind. But I am smart, Brooke. I am."

"I never said you weren't smart." Brooke's tone was like she was trying to argue.

Their mom wiped her hands on a towel and joined them in the living room. "I agree that you're smart, Ash. Definitely. All we're saying is that you need to apply yourself to schoolwork the way you apply yourself to your art."

"And soccer." Ashley stuck out her chin. "I applied myself to soccer today."

"Exactly." Brooke sounded just like Mom. "All of which will get you nowhere in life."

214

As soon as her words were out, Brooke looked like she felt bad for saying them. But she couldn't take a single one back.

"That's not very nice." Kari was washing pans at the kitchen sink.

"We're not talking to you." Brooke raised her eyes at Kari.

"Brooke!" Mom finally seemed to catch on to the meanness happening here. "Watch your tone."

"Sorry." Brooke looked at Ashley. "I'm just trying to help."

"Me, too." Kari spoke louder than the sound of the pans in the sink.

Ashley appreciated the support. She flipped her journal around to Brooke. "Look at this!" She was mad now. "It's Paris! The beautiful Awful Tower." Her eyes narrowed. "You're telling me that's a waste?"

"Eiffel Tower." Brooke was calmer now. Like she was smarter and older in every possible way. "In Paris. It's the Eiffel Tower."

Heat was pushing into Ashley's face. "Okay. So what? I'm still learning."

"Girls." Their mom's voice was kind. She gave Brooke a warning look. Then she smiled at Ashley. "Your artwork matters. So does soccer."

"Thank you." Ashley nodded. It was about time someone said so.

"Yes, Mom." Brooke wouldn't give up. "I was just saying . . . there are more important things when you're in school."

Mom nodded. She gave Ashley a kind smile. "Brooke's right about that. I remember when I was . . ." Their mom started talking about school and teachers and math. But her words seemed kind of underwater.

Suddenly Ashley's anger pushed away every other feeling. Everyone was right and she was wrong. Brooke knew better than her. Brooke always knew better. Why was Ashley drawing Paris when she had math problems waiting for her upstairs?

Again.

She stared at her artwork.

If no one wanted her to create sketches, she would forget the whole thing. Making pictures was a waste of time. That's what Brooke said. Their mom was still talking when Ashley stood and marched past both her and Brooke.

"Ashley?" Mom followed her. "I'm still talking. What are you doing?"

"This picture is garbage. It needs to go where it belongs." She walked straight to the trash can and dropped her entire journal inside.

Her mom was at her side in a blink. "Ashley! Don't you dare throw that away!"

"You can have it if you want." She glared at Brooke. "I have math to do."

"Wait." Brooke looked hurt. "I was only saying—"

The phone rang.

Her mom snatched the journal from the trash. She gave Ashley a frustrated look and then she answered it. "Hello? Yes, this is Kari's mother." She looked at Kari, who was still by the sink. "Sure. Definitely." She paused. "Just a minute."

Mom held the phone out for Kari. "It's your coach."

Their coach? Ashley turned and leaned against the refrigerator. She didn't want to miss whatever this was.

Kari took the phone. "Hello?"

Ashley watched. After a few heartbeats a smile moved up Kari's face. She nodded. "Yes. I'd like that very much." She laughed a little. "Thank you. Okay." She waited. "Yes, Saturday morning. Just like today."

Suddenly Ashley knew what had happened. Kari had made the team, after all! Coach Kelly had thought about Ashley's request and now Kari was going to play with them like before.

Ashley moved to Kari's side and held out her hand. "I need to talk to her. Please."

Kari looked like she was ready to hang up the phone. "One more thing." She said it quickly. "Ashley wants to talk to you."

Ashley had no choice. But she never thought she would hear the words coming out of her mouth.

"Coach?" She squeezed her eyes shut for a second or two. *Get it over with, Ashley. Just say it.* "Yes, this is Ashley. So, what I need to say is I'm quitting the team. I can't play this year."

"What?" Kari was standing close by. She threw her hands up. "Ashley, don't!"

"Ashley." Her mom came up on the other side of her.

Ashley didn't care what they thought. There was no going back. "I can't do this, Coach. I can't play." She took a deep breath. "Truth is, I have to focus on my studies." She had made up her mind. "Yes, I'm sure. I will cheer from the bleachers."

It was a hard decision, and when the call ended, Ashley realized something. In one afternoon, she had ended everything she was good at. And she'd given up her very last soccer season before the move to Indiana. Her mom's eyes got wide.

"Are you kidding me, Ashley?" Her mom sounded really worried this time. "You just quit soccer?"

"You said I needed to get serious." Ashley tossed her head. "That's what I'm going to do."

Kari looked like she was going to cry again. "Someone else left the team. That's why Coach Kelly put me on the roster. And now *you* quit?" She hurried off into the other room. "This is the worst day ever."

Her eyes didn't feel happy, but Ashley smiled at her mom anyway. "I'll go do my math."

Wasn't this what her parents wanted? And now Brooke had just reminded her of the thing she had already promised she would do. It was time to be serious. Time to focus on her studies.

Even if she wasn't going to be a Mighty Dolphin after all.

Ashley ran upstairs and shut her bedroom door behind her. As she grabbed her math book she decided that this wasn't her room and it wasn't Ann Arbor. It was Paris. Maybe homework was better overseas.

And if this was Paris, that meant her room could only be one place. No matter what Brooke called it.

The Awful Tower.

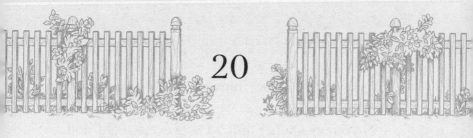

20

The Soup Kitchen

KARI

Kari couldn't think about soccer practice without her sister. Now it was Saturday and the unthinkable was about to happen.

All week Kari couldn't believe Ashley was really off the team. But her dad was taking her to the field by herself. Ashley was stuck in her math book and everything felt upside down.

Her dad gave her a weak smile. "Missing Ashley?"

"Yeah." She didn't feel like smiling. "I just wish she didn't quit."

"I understand." Her father sighed. People were doing that a lot around the Baxter house lately. "Ashley needs time to think about what she's supposed to do. I have a feeling she'll get it right. Eventually."

Kari shifted to face him better. "Brooke made her quit."

"No one made her quit." Dad gave a slight nod. "This is all Ashley."

Fifteen minutes later, when Kari was out on the field, she was still thinking about that. And of course every player came running up to her with the same question.

"Where's Ashley?"

"Did your sister really quit?"

"How are we supposed to win now?"

Lydia joined her and waved the other girls away. "Ashley is just taking some time," she told them. Then she smiled at Kari. "Glad you're on the team!"

It was the nicest thing Lydia could've said. Kari grinned, and with that she was ready to play some soccer. The most wonderful thing happened over the next two hours.

Kari got better at the game.

She ran faster than she did last time. She even passed the ball better. Her confidence was back.

She was starting to feel like she was really truly part of the team.

A Mighty Dolphin!

Two weeks of Saturday soccer practices went by and Kari couldn't believe that Ashley still hadn't changed her mind about being on the team. If she just asked, she could play with them again. Kari was sure.

Today Kari's mom and the other parents had a plan to take the girls to the Ann Arbor soup kitchen.

They were going to serve dinner to people who didn't have a home or a job. People who needed help. Kari was a little nervous about it. She had never done anything like this.

Before they went to the soup kitchen, Kari's mom offered to have the team over for an early dinner of enchilada casserole. Kari was glad. Enchilada casserole was her mother's best dinner. But of course this dinner was going to be sad and awkward for Ashley.

Sure enough, it was.

All the girls and their parents were eating off paper plates in the Baxter kitchen, everyone talking and laughing and saying what a great season the Mighty Dolphins were going to have.

And just then Ashley walked down the stairs.

No one seemed to notice her. No one except Kari. Probably because Ashley was so quiet and Kari was already nervous about seeing Ashley and hurting her feelings. Their eyes met for a second, and Ashley looked down at the ground. Then she looked at the team for a quick minute, and without saying anything she walked back upstairs.

Ashley was clearly not in the mood to visit.

This was terrible. Ashley should be downstairs with them. Talking and laughing and eating. Getting ready to go to the soup kitchen. Kari kept watching for her sister to return. But she stayed in her room, and there was nothing Kari could do to fix the problem.

Finally it came time to leave, and even then Ashley stayed away.

The soup kitchen was a place where people could eat a warm meal without paying any money. The man in charge told them that sometimes a soup kitchen served spaghetti or hamburgers or taco salad.

Today was baked chicken and mashed potatoes.

"But we can't do it without your help!" He smiled at them. "So thank you, Mighty Dolphins, for helping out tonight!"

He told them that every night different groups from the city took turns making dinner and giving it to the people. Anyone could eat at the soup kitchen, but Kari's mom told her that most of the people in line for food couldn't find a meal anywhere else.

The thought of that made Kari sad. She looked at Lydia and their teammates. They seemed sad, too. It didn't seem right. How did a person become homeless? Couldn't they just go back home again? Kari would have to ask her mom and dad later about it all.

At six o'clock the people started to come. They looked a lot like any other people. Except their clothes were dirty and older. Some of them had ripped shirts and pants. Kari was in charge of putting a dinner roll on every plate.

The people were all different types. Men and women, old and young. Some looked like families. One woman came up and smiled at her.

225

"Hello." The woman seemed nice.

"Hi." Kari handed her a roll. "Here you go."

The woman smiled. She had thick hair, sort of smushed together. "I'm Clarice." She held out her hand.

Kari shook it. "I'm Kari."

"Our names sound the same!" The lady's eyes looked a little happier. "Nice to meet you." Clarice didn't leave right away.

Kari's mother was working beside her. She was serving salad, but now she stopped and turned to the woman. "I'm Elizabeth." Her mother shook the woman's hand, too.

"You know"—Clarice's eyes looked like she was thinking of something far away—"last spring I had a house and a job. I never thought . . . I'd wind up here."

"I'm sorry." Kari's mom took hold of Clarice's hand again. "My family and I . . . we will pray for you."

"Thanks." Clarice lifted her tray of food. "That's real nice of you."

That night back at home, Kari was still thinking about the woman when her mom came in and sat on the edge of the bed. Ashley was already asleep. "I'm proud of you, for helping tonight."

"I want to do it again." Kari sat up in bed, her voice quiet. "Our whole family should help."

"Yes. I'd like that." Her mom looked at her. "Want to pray with me? For Clarice?"

"I do." Kari was glad her mom had remembered. "What do you think happened to her?"

Her mom shook her head. "Hard to tell." She smiled at Kari. "The important thing is, God knows. And He knows what she needs to find her way back again."

Kari nodded.

With that, her mom talked to God about Clarice. She asked God to work in the woman's life and keep her safe, and for her to find a job and a home again.

All of that.

Later, when her mom was gone, and Kari was trying to fall asleep, she thought about soccer and how hard it was to be part of the team without Ashley. But then she pictured Clarice. And Kari thought of something she hadn't before.

Soccer really wasn't that big of a problem, after all.

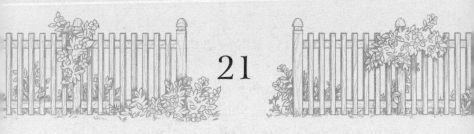

21

The Return of Ashley Baxter

ASHLEY

Ashley was miserable.

She had made a terrible decision throwing away her journal and an even worse choice quitting the soccer team. Now it was Friday after school and tomorrow was soccer practice again.

The Mighty Dolphins' first game was Tuesday after school.

Also she was tired of trying to be perfect. It wasn't working. A quick review of the last week filled Ashley's brain. When she was at home she felt like a prisoner. Captive in her math book and spelling homework.

Rapunzel locked in her tower.

At school she barely remembered to look for Samson the butterfly. She was too busy trying to listen to Miss Wilson. Today Lydia even told her the whole thing was getting annoying.

"I liked you better before." Lydia patted her on the shoulder. "See if you can find that girl again."

Ashley lay spread out on her bed. She was more miserable now than she had been five minutes ago. Maybe if she got a snack.

Downstairs she saw the rest of her family. Everyone seemed to be having a wonderful time. Something else she was missing out on. Ashley watched for a bit.

Luke and Erin were on the floor playing Memory, gathered around a bunch of turned-over cards. They were laughing. Having too much fun to notice Ashley standing there.

Great, Ashley thought. She was invisible again.

Kari was at Brittany's house for the rest of the night. And Brooke was at the movies with her friend Heather.

Ashley's parents were sitting at the dining room table. They each had a cup of coffee and they were talking, smiling. It took a minute for Ashley's mom to look her way. "Ashley. What are you doing, honey?"

In a swirling whirlwind, three weeks of trying and failing and missing out and hating her life came crashing in around her. Tears fell like a waterfall. Her words got stuck in her throat.

Mom and Dad both came closer. "Ashley, what is it?" Her mother pulled her close and held her. "Let's go upstairs and talk."

All Ashley could do was nod her head.

Her parents followed her to the room and shut the door. "Tell us, sweetheart. What is it?" Her dad sat at the desk. Mom took the edge of Ashley's bed.

"Your father and I wanted to let you live in your decisions." Mom's voice was kind. Like she felt sorry for Ashley. "We figured you'd let us know if you weren't handling it well."

So that's what had been happening? Ashley found her voice. "I've been trying so hard."

"Trying to do what?" Her dad's words came slow and steady. "Think about it, honey. What did you want out of this?"

Ashley stared at the pink blossoms on the tree outside the window. Then she looked at her math book on the bed. "I want to be perfect like Brooke." She shrugged. "That's what you told me to do."

"Oh, honey." Her mom spoke first. "That's not what we want. We asked you to care about your studies the way Brooke does. Not to *be* Brooke."

"Not at all." Dad angled his head. "You can only be you, sweetheart. There's only one Ashley Baxter. Remember that?"

Something about his statement made her worry start to lift. "I'm so bad at being Brooke." She sniffed, but her tears started up anyway. "I want to draw and play soccer and chase Samson at recess."

"Samson?" Her dad looked from Mom back to Ashley. "Who?"

"My butterfly." Ashley shook her head. "It's a long story." She took a quick breath. "I want to go to practice with Kari tomorrow and work at the soup kitchen next time the team goes and I want to be a Mighty Dolphin before it's too late."

She stood and put her hands on her hips. "I want to be me. Ashley Baxter. No one else."

Her parents didn't say anything, but they looked at each other and then at her. Ashley could tell they were trying to help and it made her feel better.

"The thing is . . ." Ashley flopped onto her bed and stared at the ceiling. "I miss being Ashley." She sat up again. "That's the truth."

Her breathing was heavy and she climbed off her bed once more. She pointed at her math book. "Sometimes I want to scream at that book." She paced a few steps toward the door and then back. "And I want someone to invent a math robot who could do the work for you while you're playing soccer or laughing with friends or drawing flower blossoms."

Her dad chuckled. "You have strong feelings on this topic."

"I do." Ashley wasn't finished. "I want to shout at that book, 'I will defeat you!' Then I would be Ashley Baxter again!" She pretended to fight invisible math problems with her pencil. "Take that . . . and that!" Even though it was a pencil, it felt like a sword to her.

Her parents watched as she waved her pencil

sword through the air. Math was the dragon and she was the princess saving the kingdom.

Princess Ashley.

At that moment there was a knock at her door. Ashley dropped her arms to her sides and opened it. She was out of breath.

Luke looked up at her. "What are you doing?"

Ashley glanced over her shoulder at the math book on her bed. "Homework."

"Oh." He looked past her to their parents. "Sounded like someone was fighting up here."

"Well." Ashley leaned to one side, thinking it over. "A little of that, too."

Luke folded his hands and looked at their dad. "Can we have ice cream? Erin and me?"

Their dad grinned. "Sure. It's Friday."

"Just one scoop." Their mom smiled. "Okay?"

"Thanks!" Luke ran off. That's all it took to make him happy.

Ashley shook her head. "He doesn't have a care in the world."

Her dad smiled. "He will. One day."

Ashley dropped to the bed next to her mother.

"All of that drama to tell you . . . I can't be Brooke, Mom." She looked at her father. "Dad, I can't do it."

She felt tears coming. But they weren't angry like they had been these past few weeks. This time, her tears were sad. Ashley put her pencil down and stared at her book. "I think I'm done." A tear fell on her jeans. She looked up at her parents.

They looked upset, too.

"Come here." Dad held his arms out, and Ashley walked straight to him. He held her for a few minutes while she cried. "Is it the move?"

Ashley thought about that for five seconds. "No . . ." She wiped a tear. "Well, yes. I don't want to move. But it's everything." She took a deep breath. "I hate not being myself."

Her dad was still holding on to her. "Was that you slaying imaginary dragons with a pencil a minute ago?"

A little sniff and Ashley pictured herself. "Yes." Her smile started all on its own. "I guess maybe that whole thing was very Ashley Baxter of me."

"Very." Her mom's laugh was kind and quiet.

"Ashley, we've told you before. No one is just like you."

Pain cramped her heart. "But you told me to be perfect."

"No." Her mom took hold of her hand. "I told you to care about your schoolwork. Like Brooke cares about hers." She ran her thumb over Ashley's hand. "Do you understand? That's all we wanted, honey."

"Sweetie." Her dad put his hands on her shoulders. So he could look right into her eyes. "Your mother and I love you for *you*. We just want you to do what's right. Do homework when you're supposed to. Be serious when it's time to be serious. Focus when you need to focus."

"So you don't want me to be another little Brooke?"

Her parents both laughed this time. "Are you kidding? This family wouldn't be the same without Ashley. Without you—just the way you are."

And right then her mom pulled something from behind her back. "Here. I believe this is yours."

Ashley gasped and jumped to her feet. Her precious journal! Her mom had saved it from the trash that terrible Saturday. Even though Ashley hadn't seen it since. "You saved it!"

"Of course." Mom handed her the book. "God made you to be an artist. And artists have to draw."

Yes! Yes, they did have to draw!

And then Ashley thought of something else. "Can we call Coach Kelly?" She looked from her mom to her dad. "So maybe I can be back on the team?" Ashley watched them share a glance. "Please. Please let me!" She'd made a big mistake quitting the Mighty Dolphins. But maybe it wasn't too late.

"They might not take you back." Her mom's words were gentle. She was just telling the truth.

"I know." Ashley nodded. "But I have to ask."

"Let's ask God about it first." Dad put his arms around her and Mom did the same thing. And then her daddy asked God for Ashley to find a way to do it all. Homework and artwork and butterflies and soccer.

It was the best prayer Ashley ever heard.

When they were done, they went downstairs

and Mom called Coach Kelly. The coach asked to talk to Ashley apparently, because her mother gave her the phone. Ashley had nerves snapping at her arms and legs, but she pressed on.

She explained the situation to Coach Kelly and she apologized for quitting.

"Well . . . the season hasn't officially started." Coach thought for a minute. "Our first game is Tuesday."

"Yes, ma'am." Ashley gulped. The answer just might be no.

Coach Kelly seemed like she was thinking hard about Ashley's question. But then all the sudden she had a smile in her voice. "The other girls would want you to play soccer with them." She waited a single heartbeat. "You really want to be on the team?"

"I do." Ashley jumped in place. "Absolutely I do."

"Okay, then." Coach Kelly laughed. "Looks like you're a Mighty Dolphin once more! Welcome back!"

"Thank you! Thank you!" Ashley thanked her coach ten more times, and when she hung up she ran to her parents and hugged them both. "I think I got carried away."

Her dad smiled down at her. "You might be right about that."

"Definitely carried away." Mom patted her head. "But that's all behind you, Ashley. It's up to you, honey. Find the balance in life. Homework and the things you love."

"Like you!" Ashley hugged her mom again. "Thank you." She grinned at her dad. "You, too, Daddy."

She went up to her room for her journal.

For a quick minute she took her pencil and pretended to fight the dragon again. The math dragon. And this time she knocked him to the ground.

"Take that!" She felt the thrill of victory. She didn't have to battle her math book anymore. She would do her homework first thing each afternoon, and she would have all the time in the world for drawing and soccer and playing with her siblings. Because she was a little wiser and because something had changed.

Ashley Baxter was back.

22

Best Sisters

ASHLEY

Soccer practice the next day made Ashley a little worried. She didn't fit in with the other girls as much as before. Lydia tried to pass her the ball three times, but twice Ashley missed it.

Which was completely not like her. *Work harder*, she told herself. *Run faster.*

But still she wasn't as good as before. She needed practice.

After they finished, Coach Kelly talked to her before the parents came. "There's a price for quitting something without thinking it through." She gave a sympathy look to Ashley. "You'll get better in time. Keep trying."

On the way home, Kari had an idea. "How about if I help you?"

Ashley tried to get her thoughts around the change here. Now it was Kari helping her. Not exactly how Ashley had pictured the season going.

But her sister only wanted to help.

So Ashley and Kari made a deal. After church the next day and after doing her homework on Monday, Ashley and Kari went out back and passed the ball a hundred times to each other.

Finally, when Tuesday's game came, Ashley felt a little more ready. The whole family loaded into the car for the big game. Their dad had even gotten the afternoon off from the hospital.

Excitement was in every breath Ashley took.

But even as she was feeling that, Brooke walked right past her without saying a single word. Ashley had a twinge of guilt. She needed to make peace with Brooke. But not now. Now it was game time.

On the ride to the field, Erin and Luke sat in the back as usual. And Kari and Brooke and Ashley sat in the middle row. But no one said a word.

"Music please, Mother." Ashley leaned forward. "Something jumpy. To get our energy up."

Their mom turned the music on and found a song with a good beat. It was the perfect energy music!

On the field before the game, as she laced up her cleats and got ready to play, Ashley couldn't stop thinking about the situation with Brooke. Her mother's words kept coming back. *Your best friends are the people around the dinner table.*

Your best friends.

Maybe if she talked to God. Ashley let the words fill her soul. *God, please help me and Brooke find our way back to being friends. I think maybe it's my fault. Or at least it is now. Your friend, Ashley Baxter.*

The game started off fast and furious.

Lydia scored a goal and then the other team scored. They were only a few minutes into the action. Parents and siblings and friends cheered and clapped and stomped their feet from the sidelines. "Might-y . . . Dol-phins . . . Might-y . . . Dol-phins."

Ashley passed the ball to Kari, and she passed it to Lydia. Three other girls took a turn with the ball, but still the Mighty Dolphins couldn't score. Same with the other team.

Halftime came and went and finally there were only a few minutes left to play. The score was still tied, one to one. Ashley just didn't feel like her old self on the field. She'd had three chances to score, but none of them had worked out.

Now Ashley was on the bench—just her and one other girl. They could do nothing to help their team from here. So Ashley did the one thing she could do.

"Go, Mighty Dolphins!" Ashley shouted. "Come on, Lydia . . . Go, Kari! Get the goal!"

Then Ashley heard something. She looked over at the stands. Brooke was on her feet cheering on the team, too. She felt a soft spot in the middle of her heart. Someone was calling her name, but all Ashley could think about was her sister.

Just then Brooke looked her way and the two of them did something they hadn't done in days. They shared a little smile.

That's when Ashley realized something. Brooke wasn't Ashley. She was Brooke. They were different, and that was actually a good thing.

Her sister was the only Brooke Baxter the world would ever have. They both were special in their own ways. They both had their own talents.

"Ashley." Coach Kelly ran down and took her by the hand. "Didn't you hear me? Go in for Rachel! We need your boot. Come on!"

This was her chance. With the fastest steps, she ran onto the field. "Let's go, Mighty Dolphins." She looked at the other girls. "We can do this!"

Ashley was playing midfield, which meant a lot of running. Coach said the team needed her boot, so that meant this was her moment. She had to score! One goal would win the whole thing.

Lydia passed to Heather, Heather to Kari, and Kari to Ashley. She wanted a breakaway, but three defenders swarmed around her. "Help!" she called out.

"Here!" It was Kari across the field near the goal.

Ashley sent the ball and watched as the defenders ran toward her sister. Maybe if she hurried toward the goal she could still get another chance. Kari passed the ball to Lydia, who passed it back to Kari.

"Score!" Coach Kelly yelled from the bench. "Kick it!"

Kari had the perfect open shot. But in a flash she sent the ball to Ashley. She could hear the fans screaming. "Mighty . . . Dolphins . . . Mighty . . . Dolphins!"

You can do this. With just one defender in front of her, Ashley dribbled to the right and kicked the ball as hard as she could.

Goal! Ashley had scored!

The other Mighty Dolphins danced and shouted and raised their hands in the air. They were winning! Ashley's boot had come in handy after all and now the team was going to win.

With teamwork, they had done it!

She looked across the field at Kari. Her sister was just standing there, a grin across her face. She gave Ashley a thumbs-up.

A minute later the game ended and Kari came running to her. "You did it!"

"No." Ashley suddenly knew. They hadn't won because of her at all. She put her arm around Kari. "*We* did it."

And so they had.

Which was just one more reason why they were best sisters.

The win called for a pizza night! So Ashley and Kari and Lydia and their families all met up at Pete's Pizza near Michigan Stadium. Everyone was still celebrating, even after they finished their dinner.

"That was the best goal!" Luke could barely sit still. "Did you hear me cheering for you?"

Ashley laughed. "Yes. You were the loudest one, Luke."

"Good." He high-fived Ashley. "That's why we won!" He looked around. "That's why you scored that goal!"

"No." Ashley looked across the table and pointed at Kari. "She's the reason we scored. Because helping each other goes both ways for sisters and for teams."

Kari grinned at her and raised her fork. "Yay, Mighty Dolphins."

Even in all the happiness, though, Brooke was quiet, sitting at the end of the table across from Ashley. She seemed sad, and Ashley promised herself that she would talk to Brooke tonight. No matter what.

But when they got home, Brooke had three friends over and all of them stayed outside playing basketball with Luke and Erin and Kari. Ashley didn't feel like intruding.

Instead she found a piece of paper from her desk drawer and sat down with her pencil. This time she wasn't going to sketch. She needed to write a letter.

She took a deep breath and put the tip of the pencil at the top of the page.

Dear Brooke,
Things have been different between us and I really don't like it. I never wanted to be annoying. It just seemed like you were trying to be my mom. But you're my sister, not my mom.
Still . . . you did say you were sorry. A lot of times. And ever since then I've been out of line.
See, I thought you and Mom and Dad wanted me to be you. Like turn into

another little you. And I realized I
cannot do that. I'm Ashley. I can only be
the best Ashley Baxter.
I am funny and crazy and loud. I love art
and soccer and butterflies. But I still want
to be your friend. Will you forgive me?
Love, your sister, Ashley

When she finished, Ashley read it over again. Yes,
that's what she wanted to say. She tucked it into the
top of her desk and waited. Later, when everyone
was getting ready for bed, Ashley found the note
and walked down the hall to Brooke's room.

Her sister was laying out her clothes for school
tomorrow, nice and neat. Ashley smiled and
watched her for a few breaths. Then she stepped
inside. "Brooke?"

Her sister turned toward her.

Ashley walked a little closer. "I've been a little
off. A little unfair to you. And kind of rude. Ever
since the Be-Like-Brooke project."

"I was just . . . trying to help." Brooke's answer
came with a wave of hurt.

Ashley held out the letter. "I know." She waited until Brooke took the folded piece of paper. "Read this. I wanted to tell you how I feel."

At first Brooke looked like she didn't want to read anything from Ashley. But then, in slow movements, she opened the paper and began to read. As she did Ashley could see little changes in her face. Her eyes got softer.

After she read the last word, Brooke looked up at Ashley. "I forgive you, Ash." She set the note down on her dresser and held out her arms. "And I'm sorry, too. I only want you to be the best you that you can be!"

Ashley closed the distance between them and the two girls hugged. Like old times. Brooke stepped back and smiled. "I want to be your friend, too."

"Forever." Ashley felt the greatest wave of peace. "Because we're moving."

"Yes." Brooke's eyes looked a bit damp. "And our best friends are right around the dinner table."

"Exactly."

The next day Brooke and Kari and Ashley played H-O-R-S-E on the basketball court with Erin and

Luke. All the kids together with everyone getting along. Too soon they would have their last day of school and they would say goodbye to their Ann Arbor friends. But Ashley was happy because once again they had each other.

And that was the best feeling in all the world.

23

All the Lasts

ASHLEY

Ashley sat on the bus, looking out the window trying to figure out where the year had gone. She was heading to school for her last day at Johnson Elementary, and everything in her wished it was the first day.

Or even the snowflake day this past winter.

Her heart felt so sad. Ashley wasn't even sure she wanted to go to school today. Because then that meant it was all real. That they were truly and actually going to move.

Kari tapped her shoulder. "What are you thinking?"

Ashley sighed. "I can't believe it's happening."

"I know . . ." Kari peered down at her backpack. "Last day . . ."

Ashley nodded, slow and certain. "Yeah." She reached for Kari's hand and held it for a few seconds. "You and I feel the same."

The bus pulled up in front of the brick building and one by one they got off. "Here goes." Kari waved at Ashley and then at Erin and Luke.

"Have a good last day!" Ashley yelled as Erin and Luke skipped off. At least the two of them seemed happy.

Ashley turned to her older sister. Kari had sad eyes. The girls shared a last look and then Kari ran off to join her fifth-grade friends. Every morning Ashley ran off the bus to her classroom. Except when she was a snowflake that one time.

But not today.

Today Ashley wanted to take her time. So she could make this final day last as long as possible.

Forever, maybe.

But then she saw Lydia. Her best school friend in the world was standing there outside the classroom door holding a sign that read: *Goodbye, Ashley! We will miss you!* And that was just the moment Lydia saw her, too.

Ashley picked up her pace and ran up to give her a big hug. "You made me a sign?" She stepped back and studied the hand-painted poster. "I love it! You're the best friend ever."

Lydia handed the poster to Ashley. "I had to send you off with a memory!" She sounded a little sad. And it was only eight in the morning. "My mom helped."

"We still have ten minutes till class starts." Ashley looked at the clock on the wall. She set her poster and backpack down. "Which means . . . we could race once around the school?"

"I don't know." Lydia laughed. "Don't you care if you get hot this early in the morning?"

"Never cared about that." Ashley was finding the fun in the day.

"Did I hear someone say they wanted to race?" It was Eric's voice.

Ashley couldn't tell if he was teasing. She turned around and there he was. "You." She lowered her eyes at him.

"You." He laughed. "Looking for a race?"

"Aren't you afraid you'll lose?" Ashley hadn't actually ever beat him. But today she had a feeling she just might.

Eric grinned. "You should be afraid. Not me."

"It's on." She got in her starting position. "To the fence and back." Longer than that and Ashley wasn't sure about her chances.

"You got it." Eric set his things down. "Okay, Baxter. Let's do this."

"Lydia! Count us off." Ashley felt sure she could beat him. She made a face in his direction. "Oh . . . and it's not Baxter. It's Ashley!"

Lydia did her part. "Three . . . two . . . one—"

"No!" Miss Wilson stepped out of the classroom and interrupted the race before it started. "No racing now. It's time for class." She motioned for them to get into the room. "Maybe at recess!"

Ashley felt the thrill leave her heart. "But, Miss Wilson . . . I was going to win. For the first time."

"Sorry. We have a lot to do." She sounded happy. "It's the last day of school!"

They all headed into the classroom.

And what a last day it was.

Every hour was something different. A round of the hot potato game first, and then one of the moms brought in cupcakes. After that, they cleaned their desks, and when they were all finished Miss Wilson had them sit down again.

"I have a surprise!" She pulled up a box from behind her desk. "Memory books. One for each of you."

When Ashley got hers, she opened it and her soul soared. Inside were pictures from the fall party, the field trip to the Christmas concert, the snowflake project, the Valentine's party and even one photo of Samson the butterfly.

The perfect souvenir for her years at Johnson Elementary.

Before she started taking the memory book around to have her friends sign it, Ashley walked to Miss Wilson's desk. She held the book up. "Will you write in mine first?" Ashley set the book down in front of her teacher. "I know I haven't been the easiest student."

"No." Miss Wilson laughed as she picked up

Ashley's memory book. "Not the easiest."

"But I will say"—Ashley smiled—"you are my favorite teacher. And I won't forget you."

The start of tears showed up in Miss Wilson's eyes. "I won't forget you, either, Ashley." She smiled. "I wish everyone loved life the way you do."

Finally, Ashley thought, *someone who understands me.* She nodded. "I wish that, too."

Again Miss Wilson laughed, but then she signed Ashley's book. Next Ashley took it to Lydia, who she was going to miss forever and always.

During recess Ashley and Lydia stayed with the other girls and signed memory books. Ashley really wanted to race Eric. If she was ever gonna beat him, it was today. Because today was full of lasts. Which meant it was the last time Ashley *could* beat him. So of course she would.

The rest of the day sped by in fast motion. And then, like a million days before this one, the bell rang. But this was the last time, so Ashley didn't jump up and run out of the room like the other kids. She and Lydia stayed right there.

Maybe they could pretend it wasn't the bell and it wasn't the last day.

And pretend that her family wasn't moving away.

Ashley didn't say anything. She didn't have to. Lydia, either. They stared at Miss Wilson, who was facing the blackboard. The message read, *Have a Good Summer*.

With big circles, Miss Wilson erased the words until the board was clean again. Ready for another fourth-grade class when summer was over.

Miss Wilson turned around, and she looked surprised. "Girls! It's summer. Go play!"

"No thank you." Ashley held her head high. "I just wanna sit for a little bit more. If that's okay." Ashley looked out the window, and back at her teacher. "I'm going to miss the view."

"Me, too." Lydia looked at her and smiled. "You got me in trouble a hundred times, Ashley Baxter." She took a slow breath. "But I only wanted to sit by you."

Miss Wilson seemed to understand. Because she started packing up her desk. Just then Ashley saw something near the classroom entrance. She turned and there was Eric. Leaning against the doorframe.

"Hey, Baxter." He grinned. "How about that race?" He raised his eyebrows. "Our last chance, right?"

Ashley was on her feet in an instant. "Come on, Lydia. You don't want to miss this."

Both girls grabbed their things. Ashley waved goodbye to Miss Wilson once more. "I'll visit sometime." Ashley pushed back the sadness. "My dad said to tell everyone that."

"Okay!" Miss Wilson waved, too. "Be yourself, Ashley. And do your homework!"

Ashley laughed. "I will. Have a great summer, Miss Wilson. Thanks for everything."

Outside, Ashley set her things down on the ground and lined up next to Eric. "Lydia . . . count us off, please."

Once more Lydia did the countdown. "Three . . . two . . . one . . . *Go!*"

Ashley and Eric took off across the grassy field toward the fence. Most of the students were gone by now, but a few cheered them on. Just like Ashley thought, her feet were faster than ever before.

She and Eric kept right at the same pace all the way to the fence. But on the way back she got a little ahead and a little more and Ashley pushed herself even more. *Faster! Faster! You can do this!* she told herself.

Just a little ways more and then . . . Yes! Ashley won! She actually won! One of the boys from their class yelled, "Eric, you let her win!"

"No!" He was out of breath. He leaned over his knees and Ashley did the same. "She . . . she beat me! Fair and square."

This was how Ashley wanted to end this day. Running as fast as she could with the wind in her hair. She was having too much fun to be sad.

"You did it." Lydia gave her a high five. "You actually beat Eric Powers!"

Across the field Ashley saw Kari and Erin and Luke boarding the school bus. She only had a couple more minutes.

Eric had his breath now. He came to her and held out his hand. "Nice race, Ashley."

She stopped in her tracks. Then she took hold

of his hand and shook it. But all she could think about was one thing. For the first time all year, Eric had called her by her name. He called her Ashley.

She smiled. "Thank you."

His smile faded a little. "Hope your move goes okay."

"Me, too." Ashley would even miss Eric Powers. She knew that now.

"See ya sometime . . ." His smile was the nicest it had ever been. "Bye." He picked up his backpack and walked across the field.

"Bye, Eric . . ." Ashley called after him. "See ya."

She would see Lydia on Saturday at their last soccer game. But she wouldn't see Eric Powers again. Ashley hugged Lydia and then she ran after her siblings. This time as she ran, she had just one hope in her heart.

She hoped that the wind would dry her tears.

The soccer party at the Baxter house was wrapping up. Lots of Ashley's teammates had said goodbye. Each of them told Ashley and Kari that they'd miss them next year.

"Maybe we'll come for a game," Ashley said at least eight times. But already Ashley knew that she and Kari would be playing soccer with their new friends on a new team.

"You know what I think." Ashley came up to her mom as another two girls and their families left. "I think we won't probably come for a visit next season."

"Maybe not." Mom nodded, sadness in her eyes. "But you never know, Ash."

"I do know." Ashley waved at the walls around them. "This is all about to be a think of the past."

Her mother looked at her. "Do you mean a *thing* of the past?"

Ashley thought for a minute. "Actually I like 'think of the past.' I'll only remember all this when I think about it."

"Oh. I see" Her mom smiled. "I like that."

Lydia said goodbye at the end, but she and her mom were coming by tomorrow to say one last goodbye. For now Ashley and Kari had to finish packing up their clothes.

Everything in their room was packed in a big box.

261

Kari's teddy bear and her sand dollar and dream collage board. Ashley's soccer ball and cleats and the little book on encouragement from her mom.

After tomorrow, Ashley would only have the memories of these years in Ann Arbor and the time in Miss Wilson's class, Eric Powers and the Mighty Dolphins and Lydia . . . all of it would be a part of yesterday.

Nothing more than a think of the past.

24

Saying Goodbye

ASHLEY

Ashley woke to the sound of the truck backing up her driveway. The beeping was worse than any alarm ever. Because the loud noise meant only one thing.

It was time to leave.

Bare walls. Empty dresser drawers. And a cleaned-out closet. The only things left in the house Ashley loved so much.

She sat up, rubbed her eyes, and looked over at Kari's bed. But Kari wasn't there. Ashley jumped up and ran down the hall to Brooke's room. She wasn't there, either! Next she ran to Luke and Erin's room, flung open the door, and . . . gone!

All of them.

Had her parents and siblings moved without her? Ashley brushed her hands over her eyes again. No, that wasn't possible. The moving truck was still out there making that terrible beeping.

"Um . . . Ashley!"

She jumped around to see Brooke. "You're here!" Ashley clutched her heart so the beating would slow down a little. "I thought everyone left!"

"We're eating breakfast." Brooke smiled at her. "Come on."

Ashley followed her oldest sister. The two of them were so much closer now. Dad said hard times could do that to people. Make them better. Closer.

Downstairs the whole family was eating bagels and cream cheese and blueberries. Brooke laughed as they filled their plates. "You didn't really think we left . . . did you?"

"Well." Ashley tried to wink. But both eyes closed instead of just one. Which made her laugh out loud. "Not really. I mean . . . Okay, for a few minutes, maybe."

All the kitchen and living room furniture was

already in the truck, so they sat in a circle in the middle of the dining room floor.

Their dad talked to God for them, asking that they would make as many memories and good friends in Bloomington as they had here in Ann Arbor. "We're all a little sad." He looked at each of the kids and landed on Ashley. "But it will get better. I promise."

Mom nodded. "It's an adventure now. Just us Baxters."

Ashley liked the sound of that. She took a bite of her bagel. They would be okay. They really would. But first she had to say goodbye to Lydia.

Something she had been dreading for weeks.

When breakfast was finished, Brooke had an idea. "Let's go to the tree house."

Ashley got excited. "How about we get markers? So we can say our last tree marks."

"Last remarks?" Her dad chuckled. "You definitely keep us entertained, Ashley."

She smiled. "You're welcome." Her shoulders moved up and down. "I think you're right about last remarks. That's what I meant."

"Actually, maybe your way is better." Her dad grinned. "'Last tree marks.' Sounds about right."

Ashley grinned at her father, and then all five of them ran outside and climbed into the tree house.

For the last time.

When they were all seated in a circle on the highest level, Ashley remembered something. "We haven't been out here all together since we found out we were moving."

"That's true." Kari looked at her hands and then at each of them. "It's sad. That we're leaving."

"It is." Erin nodded and Luke did the same. It was the first time he seemed less than excited about what was happening.

"And this . . ." Brooke pressed her fingers under her eyes. She did a little cough. "This is our last time to be here in the tree house."

Ashley thought about something else. Someone had bought their house. So that meant some other kids were going to have the tree house soon.

Silence hung in the air as they all looked out the windows into their backyard. Ashley closed her eyes and inhaled. The summer smells of her favorite trees and flowers and their own piece of sunshine filled her lungs. For a few seconds she held her breath.

Like maybe she could take a little bit of Ann Arbor with her.

"I . . . uh . . . I brought the markers." Kari held up a few colorful pens. She passed them out. "Everyone write something on the walls. A message to whoever gets this tree house next."

Erin took a purple one. "I like this." With great care, she wrote her name on one wall. The letters were maybe an inch high. "Now everyone will know this used to be my place."

Kari wrote her name and a verse from the Bible in her own words: God has good plans for you. Whoever you are.

It was Brooke's turn. She wrote her name and then this: Don't forget to have fun. That's what tree houses are for.

Luke just wrote his name and a smiley face. "That says it all for me."

They laughed, and Luke did, too.

It was Ashley's turn. She took a blue marker and

found a bare spot on the far wall. The one with the biggest window. She wrote her name and then something she'd been thinking about for a few minutes. *Don't try to be like everyone else. God made just one you. P.S.—Take care of this tree house. It has love in the walls.*

Then on the next wall Ashley made a quick drawing of the Baxter children.

She tried to add a little something special about each of them. Erin's glasses. Luke's spiky hair. Kari's pretty smile. Brooke's big eyes. And for Ashley, a pencil in her hand.

Princess Ashley, fighting math dragons.

Saving the kingdom one last time.

Lydia and her mom pulled up out front ten minutes later. By then the kids were all back inside the house. Ashley peered out the door and saw Lydia climb out of the car.

"I hate this." She pressed her forehead into the wall. "How am I supposed to say goodbye?"

The message was for her and God's ears only. But Brooke must've heard, because she came up and put her hand on Ashley's back. "With a full heart." Brooke's voice was the kindest ever. "That's how."

Then Brooke walked back into the kitchen with everyone else. Because goodbyes sometimes had to happen without a lot of people watching. Lydia and her mom came up the sidewalk and Ashley met them on the porch.

Already Lydia was crying. "I don't want to say goodbye."

"Me, too." Tears sprang into Ashley's eyes. She hugged Lydia and held her for a long time. "It's going to be a boring summer in Bloomington. Without you."

"I was just telling my mom that. A whole summer without you will feel like forever." Lydia sniffed and smiled. "I'll miss all our fun adventures. I can't believe you're really going."

Ashley's mom stepped out onto the porch. "We have to go, sweetheart." She hugged Lydia's mom. "Thanks for coming."

"I promised her one more goodbye." Lydia's mom looked heartbroken. Because that's how moms look when their kids are sad.

They didn't have much time. Ashley hugged Lydia once more. "Thanks for being my friend. Even when it was hard." Ashley's words got stuck in her throat. She coughed a little.

"Thanks for being mine." Lydia laughed even as a few new tears fell down her face. "You are one of a kind, Ashley Baxter. No one will ever be as fun as you."

They laughed and cried and then laughed again. But there was no way around what was next.

It was time to say goodbye.

Lydia and Ashley hugged once more, and this time, both girls cried. Ashley wondered if her heart would break in half. Every wonderful memory with Lydia circled in her heart and reminded her of the worst thing.

All of it was over.

"You'll visit, right?" Lydia stepped back. Her mom put her hand on her shoulder.

"We will." Ashley wasn't sure when or how often. But somewhere down the road they would visit. They had to, because otherwise this goodbye wouldn't just be sad.

It would be impossible.

Finally, Lydia exhaled. She dried her face with the palms of her hands. "Write me. Or call if you can!" Lydia squeezed Ashley's hands.

"I will. You, too." Ashley squeezed back and nodded. "Bye, Lydia."

"Bye, Ashley."

Lydia and her mom walked to their car and once she was buckled in, Lydia waved out the window. Ashley waved, too. All the way until Lydia's mom drove their car around the corner.

Then she collapsed against her mother. "This . . . is so hard."

"I know." Her mom held her warm and close. "I'm sorry."

They stayed that way for a while, until Ashley felt strong enough to stand up on her own. She dried her face and tried to smile at her mom. "It can't get harder than this."

"No. Probably not." She smoothed Ashley's hair. "Go get your backpack."

Ashley turned and headed inside the house. It was quiet and empty. It was their house . . . but at the same time, it wasn't. It looked different without the furniture and without her family. Without the sounds of them living and loving each other here.

The spaces looked strange.

She ran her hand along the wall and made her way into the kitchen. It was the place where they had cooked pancakes and pizza and apple pie. Here was where they had shared a thousand birthdays and dinners and funny stories.

Next Ashley walked to the living room. Where they once played Old Maid and Scrabble and talked till late in the night, the room where their dad played his guitar.

Memories lived in every inch of the house. But they wouldn't stay here. They would go with Ashley and her sisters and brother. They would stay with her parents, too.

They would stay in their hearts.

Ashley walked up the stairs. Each step felt more difficult than the last. This was another part she didn't want to do.

Say goodbye to her room.

Ashley opened the door. It was empty now. The special part of the house she and Kari shared was just an open space now. Just faded squares on the walls from where posters and pictures used to be.

Ashley grabbed her backpack, flung it over her shoulder. Then she lowered herself to the floor, cross-legged.

"I wondered where you were." Kari's voice sounded behind her.

Ashley turned around. "I had to say goodbye." She looked around the room again and pressed her fingers into the familiar carpet.

"Remember in kindergarten when I split the room down the middle with tape?" Kari's voice was light. Like she wanted to hold on to the happy times they'd shared here.

"Yes!" Ashley had almost forgotten that. "You said I couldn't cross over to your side!"

Kari laughed. "Mom found out and we both had to scrub the sticky stuff off the window and wall!"

The memory made Ashley smile. "We became even better friends over that. Something that should've torn us apart brought us together."

After a minute, Kari dropped down to the floor beside Ashley. "We had some good times in this room."

"We did." Ashley put her arm around Kari. The two of them, side by side. For now, for these last few moments, this was still their room. And Ashley wanted to sit here as long as she could.

A knock came at the door. They both turned to see their dad. His eyes looked red. "You girls ready? Everyone's in the van."

Ashley nodded and stood. She helped Kari to her feet. "I guess." Ashley would never be ready, but she didn't have a choice.

"Okay, then." Their dad walked back down the hallway.

Ashley and Kari grabbed hands, and, without saying another word, they left their room and walked downstairs to the front door. Kari kept walking, but Ashley stopped.

One more time, she looked back inside. "Good-bye, house . . ." She put her hand on the door-frame. Then, with every inch of her strength, Ashley turned away and walked to the car.

Their dad locked up the house. Then he climbed into the front seat and they pulled away. Ashley watched her house for as long as she could. Kari and Brooke did the same thing.

Their mom, too.

When they turned the corner, their dad looked in the rearview mirror at the rest of them. "Get ready, Bloomington. The Baxters are coming for you!"

Ashley was still sad. Tears streamed down her face again. But there was something exciting about the way their dad's words sounded. They were moving to a new city with a new school and new friends. A new house and a new soccer team.

No telling what else might be there.

They got on the interstate and Ashley pulled her journal from her backpack. She opened it to the page she liked best. The drawing of the Baxter house in Ann Arbor.

She loved every brick, every shutter, every window. The mailbox and roof. All of it. Ashley would remember every detail for always.

But somewhere in Bloomington, Indiana, stood another house. The one they were going to move into. Dad and Mom said it had a porch and a stream out back and a garden with roses. Their Realtor had found it for them. Mom said she thought it was the prettiest house she'd ever seen.

Ashley believed her. Her mom always told the truth.

Quiet words to God ran through Ashley's heart. *God. I'm nervous about all this. And I'm sad to say good-bye. But I trust my dad and mom. And I trust You. I don't know what's ahead in Bloomington, but I have a feeling it'll be good. Like Mom always says. "You never leave us. Great is your faithfulness."*

She leaned her head against the window. The trees rushed by as Michigan disappeared behind them. But even so something inside Ashley couldn't help but feel like the best was yet to come. That just maybe the most exciting years of her life were waiting for her in Bloomington. Ashley would go to middle school there and high school.

Bloomington was where life would begin. Not just for her, but for all of them. The Baxter children. She took one last look at her sketch of the old house, and then an idea hit her.

A long sigh slipped between her lips, and finally she did what she had to do. She closed the journal. One day soon she would open it again. She would turn to a fresh, crisp, blank page and she would draw her new house. The one they were about to meet.

Ashley set her journal in her backpack and stared out the window. A smile lifted her lips, even as her tears were still wet on her cheeks. There were so many possibilities ahead in Bloomington. And suddenly Ashley had a thought that surprised her.

She could hardly wait.

Because this time they weren't just taking an adventure together. They were doing something only a family could do.

The Baxters were finding home.

Best Family Ever

• Family Activity Guide •

As the Baxters say, your best friends are the people around the dinner table every night. Family time is such an important part of the day, a chance to share your life, talk through your feelings, and have fun with one another! Here are some questions to discuss with your family and also a list of activities to do together.

Questions for Around the Dinner Table

1. Did you or do you have a tree house? What was/is it like?

2. Who is/was your best friend in school? What's your favorite thing about that friend?

3. God makes each person special. Tell three things that are special about you.

4. Have you ever moved? What did you like about moving? What was the hardest part?

5. Where would you like to go for vacation? Why? What would you like to do on that vacation?

6. What does it mean that your best friends are the ones sitting around the dinner table? Can you give an example of this in your life? If not, what could you do to make best friends out of your family members?

7. Which do you like more—drawing or writing?

8. If you were going to draw a picture of your week, what would it look like?

9. If you were going to write a story about your family, what would you call it?

10. If you could ask God one question, what would you ask Him?

Activities with Your Family and Friends

1. Make cookies with your family. Decorate them and share a plate with a neighbor.

2. Draw something that represents your day, and do this every day for a week.

3. Write a paragraph about your day, and do this every day for a week.

4. Leave your electronics at home and explore your neighborhood. Then draw a picture of what you like most.

5. Write a short story about something imaginary that could happen on your street.

6. Offer to help someone at home with schoolwork or a chore. How did that feel?

7. Plan a breakfast party for your family and help cook.

Did You Know?

Ann Arbor is so cold in the wintertime that the parks department sprays water on open fields to create neighborhood ice rinks.

The average person moves eleven times in his or her lifetime.

It takes eight years of college education to become a doctor.

The Eiffel Tower in Paris is 1,063 feet tall.

A butterfly spends up to twenty-one days in a cocoon.

Turn the page for a sneak peek at
Finding Home.

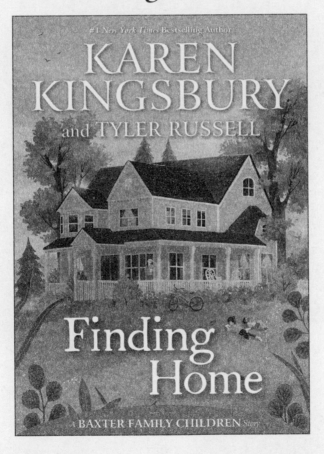

Far from Home

ASHLEY

Ashley Baxter tapped her foot on the car floor. Every interstate sign they passed meant just one thing. She and her family were getting farther away from Michigan. Farther away from her best friend, Lydia. Ashley slumped into her seat and stared out the window. All she wanted was to get out of this hot, stuffy car and run the other way. Back to Ann Arbor.

The only place she would ever call home.

She looked down. A blob of ketchup from lunch had landed smack in the middle of her white T-shirt, and the rest-stop bathroom paper towel had only made it worse. Her shorts were bunched up and the truth was, she'd had enough of this whole moving trip.

Ashley put her hands on her hot cheeks and leaned into the space between her parents in the front seat. "I'm feeling faint back here." She blew at her damp bangs. "Are you sure it can't get any colder in this place?"

"That's all we've got, sweetheart." Dad glanced over his shoulder.

A huff came from Ashley's lips as she sat back again. Fine.

Her parents said the drive to their new house in Bloomington, Indiana, was only six hours away. But it might as well have been a hundred and six. Ashley took out her sketchbook and studied her last picture. The one she had drawn as they left their old neighborhood.

A picture of their house. Their home.

Ashley breathed deep and rested her head against the window. She closed her eyes. Why did they have to move, anyway? She thought about asking, but she didn't want to ruin her family's happy mood. So she kept the thought to herself. A quick blink and she stared out the windshield. The trees along the side of the highway looked familiar. Her heart lit up. Maybe Dad had turned the car around at the last stop and he was secretly taking them back to Michigan. A smile tugged at her lips. It was possible, right?

A few seconds passed and the scenery looked different again. The truth hit hard. They weren't going back.

Not ever.

"Ten minutes!" Dad peeked back at Ashley and the other kids through the rearview mirror. His eyes twinkled and his smile was the happiest of anyone's all day. "Who's excited?"

"Woo-hoo! Me!" Brooke's shout came first. She was the oldest Baxter child and she sat against the opposite window. Kari, a few years younger, sat between them. Brooke bounced a little. "I can hardly wait."

Ashley frowned. No surprise Brooke was happy about all this. She didn't have a best friend back home. No one like Lydia. From the rear seat, their two youngest siblings—Erin and Luke—clapped and cheered.

Ashley sighed. "I'm happy for you, Brooke." She turned so she could see Erin and Luke better. "And for both of you. My sweet young innocent siblings."

"It's gonna be great." Dad took hold of their mother's hand.

Ashley breathed out a long breath. *Calm, Ashley. Be calm.* Maybe Dad was onto something. Wherever they were going, at least they had each other.

A big map stretched out across Mom's legs. A thick yellow marker line ran all the way down from Ann Arbor to Bloomington and it finished with a huge red circle labeled *Home!*

Ashley stared at that word. *Home.* What did that mean, really? If her family was leaving home, how could they also be *heading* home?

Mom's eyes got wide, and her voice was a happy squeal. "Take this exit, John. North Walnut Street . . . We're here!"

They left the highway and turned onto a city street. The trees were tall and thick with lush canopies of green leaves. Like something from one of their summer vacations.

"Okay, kids!" Dad looked in the rearview mirror again. "This is downtown Bloomington!"

"Look!" Mom pointed at one of the buildings. "There's a coffee shop and a farmers' market. And see down there . . . a little theater." Her voice trailed off.

The city reminded Ashley of commercials for Disneyland. Old brick buildings, bright-colored flowers, and neatly trimmed bushes. Families walked along both sides of the street, everyone smiling. Like something from a movie.

A butterfly feeling came into Ashley's stomach. Was she afraid or excited? She couldn't tell. The place looked special. A spot she might want to visit. The butterflies flew all the way up to her heart and a thrill ran through her.

Lydia would love this place.

They drove past a sign that read: SUNSET HILLS ADULT CARE HOME. The sign had an arrow pointing to a skinny street. Ashley tried to see what was down there, but their van was moving too fast. She liked the name. *Sunset Hills.*

After a while they turned down a country road that stretched into wide green fields and rolling hills. The houses here had open spaces around them. Very different from their neighborhood back home.

Kari began to bite her fingernails. She did that when she was nervous. "We . . ." Her voice sounded shaky. "We're going to live in the wilderness?"

"No, honey." Mom looked back and smiled. "This is the country. Our new house is in the country."

This detail made Erin and Luke and Brooke release another round of cheers. Luke patted Ashley and Kari on their shoulders. "I knew I was going to like it here!" He jumped in his seat a few times. "I'm Christopher Robin! With my own Hundred Acre Wood! All to myself!"

Erin giggled. "If you're Christopher Robin, I'm Piglet. Cause I'm little."

"I'll be Owl." Brooke raised her hand. "I'm the oldest."

Next to Ashley, Kari's smile turned sort of dreamy. "Then I'll be Winnie-the-Pooh! I can help you explore, Luke."

They all talked at once about how there would be ponds and toads and bunnies. Places to take walks and catch fish and look at the stars. A sigh built in Ashley's heart and escaped through her lips. "I guess that makes me Eeyore."

"Nah!" Dad did a half laugh from the front. "You'll be Tigger. One of a kind."

"And fun, fun, fun!" Kari grinned at her.

"Hmm." Ashley tossed that around in her brain. Before she could stop herself, she smiled. "Tigger is definitely better than Eeyore."

"Much better!" Kari put her arm around Ashley's shoulders. "Plus we can't be sad forever."

Dad turned the car left onto a long driveway and nodded at the house up ahead. "This is it! Our new home!"

"Wow!" Mom clapped. "It's beautiful."

The van slowed to a stop and Dad checked the road behind them for a few seconds. "Our moving truck should be here any minute."

Ashley studied the house. It was tall and white. Like a place where Pollyanna or Anne of Green Gables might live. A long porch stretched around it, and orange and yellow flowers decorated the front. On either side of the house there stood trees that looked perfect for drawing.

When they reached the house, Dad parked and everyone climbed out. Kari and Brooke ran up the steps onto the porch, while Erin and Luke took off for the backyard. Their parents smiled and headed for the front door.

Ashley crossed her arms and stayed planted near the car. She looked the house up and down and pursed her lips. "You're pretty." She squinted. "But you're not home."

Mom noticed her hanging back. "Ashley! Come on!" She held her hands up high. "What do you think?"

"I think"—Ashley whispered to herself—"it

looks like a castle." She walked up to her mom. "It's a bit big." She turned her head to one side. "I'm not seeing an actual house here. Maybe at a different angle . . ."

Mom stooped down so they were eye to eye. "I see what you mean. It's not the same as our other house."

"No. It's . . . different." Ashley bit her lip. "Which can be—"

"Good?" Mom finished Ashley's sentence and placed a loose piece of hair behind Ashley's ear.

"I don't think so." Ashley felt tears sting her eyes. "But maybe. Someday."

"Atta girl. Come on." Mom took Ashley's hand and led her into the house. "You're going to love it."

Inside, Kari raced up to them. She was out of breath. "Ash! Come see our room!" Then she took off up the stairs.

Ashley had no choice. She took hold of the wooden banister and trudged along behind her sister. One slow step at a time. At the top, she turned down the hallway. She walked past what looked like Erin's room on one side and Luke's on the other. Then Kari stepped out of the second door just ahead. "Wait till you see what I found! Come on!" She pulled Ashley into the room. It was a lot bigger than the one in Michigan and the ceiling was taller.

Also Ashley noticed a small purple stain on the carpet. At the other end of the room stood a window as tall as their whole room and beneath it a built-in bench.

"Isn't it perfect?" Kari ran to the window. "You could even sketch here! Come look."

"Hmm." Ashley took her time. When she reached the window she wrinkled her nose. "It's too big. No privacy."

"No it's not. It's beautiful. It looks like a princess window!" Kari pressed her nose against the glass. "Plus . . . we have so much space out there! Look at all we can see."

Ashley made a face. Five houses could fit in the front yard. "It's like a park." Ashley stared out the window. The only neighbors were very far away. The place really was the Hundred Acre Wood. "It feels like a hotel." She stepped back and crossed her arms. "Not a home."

"Don't be silly." Kari stared out again. "It's the best view in the world. Our own little kingdom." Kari had never sounded happier.

Ashley frowned. Who wanted to live in a lonely kingdom? And what sort of girl wanted a castle for a house? Her regular old bedroom was perfect and it was all she could think about. All she wanted.

Kari pulled Ashley to the closet and they stepped inside. "We could have a sleepover in here alone. It's huge!"

"True." Ashley kind of liked this idea. But not enough to smile. The best sleepovers were back home in Michigan.

"Look!" Kari put her hand on the closet wall and there, etched in pen, was a message. Kari read it out loud. "To the next person who lives here. This is the best room ever. Sorry about the carpet. My friend spilled purple nail polish. Love, Susie Macon."

"No wonder the place doesn't feel right." Ashley lifted her chin. "It belongs to some girl named Susie."

"Girls!" It was their dad calling from downstairs. "Come down!" He paused. "We have a problem."

Great. Ashley's shoulders sank. First she and Kari were being forced to live in someone else's room. And now there was another problem.

Downstairs Dad told them the news. "I'm glad we had the phone hooked up early. I just heard from the movers. Their truck broke down." He frowned. "They won't be here till tomorrow."

"Excuse me." Ashley raised her hand. "What if someone steals our stuff? I have important things in there."

"My best hairbrush is on that truck." Brooke crossed her arms.

Before Dad could answer, a thought came to Ashley. She cleared her throat. "You know, Dad . . . maybe this is a sign." She smiled politely. "We could tell the movers to turn around and we could meet them back home. Forget the whole thing."

The other kids started talking all at once until Dad let out a whistle. "Easy." He waved his hands a few times. "Everyone relax. We aren't going back. We'll order pizza and sleep on the living room floor."

"Pizza!" Luke cheered.

"And in the morning we can paint the back porch! That'll keep us busy till the movers come." Dad made it sound like this was a great change of plans.

Mom laughed. "Wasn't how I pictured tonight going, but it'll be a memory."

Then Dad walked to her and wrapped his arms around her. "Elizabeth, my love . . . we're home."

"Yes." Mom put her head on his shoulder. "Yes we are."

Watching them made Ashley feel a little better. But they were wrong about one thing. This definitely wasn't home.

The pizza arrived and after dinner they explored some more and then they made their beds on the floor out of sweaters and pillows from the car. Ashley closed her eyes and tried to sleep, but the noises kept her awake. First, a chatty owl and then a crying wind, which made the house creak. Suddenly a howl shook the air. Ashley sat straight up.

Wolves! Right outside the back door!

Everyone else was asleep. The moon through the windows cast strange shadows on the carpet. The house was empty and lonely and scary. Definitely scary. What if the wolf got inside?

"Dad." She whispered in his direction, but there was no response. She lay back down on her side and pulled her knees up close to her chin.

Dear God. It's me, Ashley. I'm in this new house. And I think there's a wolf outside. The moon was bright enough for Ashley to find her sketchbook. With quick pencil strokes she drew a different kind of wolf. Friendly and funny-looking. Then she waited.

The wolf was quiet now. *Okay, God. I know different isn't always bad. But please can I go back home? Someday soon? Thank You. Good night.*

Ashley didn't hear a response. But she felt better. God was always listening. Even still, the noises started again. Ashley opened her eyes and stared at the ceiling. She'd never be happy in this house. Not with the chatty owl. Not with the howling wolf.

And not when they were so very far from home.

Painting the Porch

ASHLEY

The morning sun shone through the window, and Ashley yawned. Mom's coffee smell filled the air, same as it used to every morning back home. Ashley sniffed and scrunched up her nose. The smell seemed strange in this big empty place.

She groaned and sat up. Not only was the carpeted floor hard and bumpy, but that crazy owl had hooted all night.

"Morning." Brooke sounded tired. She leaned up on her elbow. "How'd you sleep?"

"Not good." Ashley blinked a few times. "The wolves kept me awake."

Brooke sat straight up. "Wolves?"

Just then a loud beeping came from outside. Ashley gasped. "The truck!" She ran toward the front door and swung it wide open. The yellow moving van was backing down the long driveway with Dad guiding it closer to the house.

"Our things!" Kari joined them, and she and Brooke jumped around.

Ashley crossed her arms. She didn't want her things here. She wanted them back in Michigan. Where they belonged.

"It's finally real!" Brooke took in a deep breath. "Indiana air is the best!"

Ashley sniffed. The scent was grass and trees and hay. Like the Michigan State Fair. She wrinkled her nose. Home wasn't supposed to smell like a fair. Ashley turned to their mother. "Are we still painting the back porch?"

"We are!" Mom grinned. "Or I should say . . . you kids are." She moved to go back inside. "Oh . . . and your dad picked up breakfast sandwiches and paper plates. They're in the kitchen." She kissed Ashley and Brooke on the tops of their heads. "Come eat."

The other kids were awake and Dad joined them

for their first breakfast in the new house. They got to sit on the kitchen counter, which was usually not allowed. Already Luke was talking about the pond out back on their actual property. "It's perfect for tadpoles!"

Dad nodded. "The yard is bigger than I thought." He winked at Luke. "A lot to explore."

"Yeah!" Luke had the cutest grin. "I can't wait."

Brooke talked about how her room had the prettiest view for reading and Erin said she wanted to look for wildflowersout back. Kari pointed to the big window in the living room. "I can already imagine our Christmas tree right there."

Mom's voice was hopeful. "I prayed you kids would wake up seeing something good here."

Ashley drummed her fingers on her knee and looked around. *Something good . . . hmm.* Nothing came to mind.

Dad turned to her. "What about you, sweetie? So far, what's the best thing about being here?"

She thought for a minute. Slowly an idea hit her. "Maybe . . . painting." The idea made her feel a little better. "We get to paint the porch today."

She sat a little straighter. "Which is the best activity for an artist."

"I like it." Dad laughed. "I have five brushes and a few buckets of white paint waiting out back." He clapped his hands together one time. "Who's with Ashley? Hands in."

Ashley and her siblings giggled. They jumped down from the counter and formed a circle. They each put one hand in the middle, all together, like a sports team.

Dad and Mom added their hands. "One . . ." Dad smiled at the group. "Two . . . three . . ."

The whole family yelled, "Team!" Then they raised their hands in the air.

"Everyone out back." Dad grabbed the last sandwich. Then he turned to their mom. "Elizabeth, I think we're going to love it here." He tipped his baseball cap. "All right, Ash. Let's go!" He squatted low and Ashley hopped on his back. "Porch Paint Express . . . here we come!" He carried her to the front door. "I need a whistle! Come on!"

"Tooot Toooot!" Ashley pumped her fist twice in the air. She laughed out loud because something wonderful was finally happening in Bloomington.

They were having an adventure.

Sweat dripped down Ashley's face as she rested her paintbrush and looked behind her. They were getting it done. Almost two hours into painting and half the porch was bright white. She wiped her forehead with her sleeve.

Her siblings were slowing down, and Luke kept talking about the pond. Next to Ashley, Kari was painting about half as fast as before. "It's hot." She fanned herself a few times, and tugged at the collar of her shirt, like she would do anything to get some fresh air. "I didn't think it would take so long."

Even with the heat, Ashley wasn't tired. She loved this job. Of course paint wouldn't make the place a home. But still, this was fun. She had never painted an actual building before. She dragged the brush slow and steady over the soft old wood. Every inch the brush touched turned bright white.

Like it was brand new.

Dad told them whoever lived here before had sanded off the old color and probably meant to paint it. But they never did. Maybe the family was too busy cleaning up Susie's spilled nail polish. Whatever the reason, they left a perfect opportunity for the Baxters.

A way to actually enjoy their first day in the new house.

Ashley focused. *Dip the brush, wipe it on the inside of the can, spread the paint on the smooth worn wood.* She had a system now. She bit her lip. *Dip. Wipe. Spread.*

Kari stopped and watched her. "You're good at this!"

"Thanks." Ashley felt her heart light up. "It's easy. Dip. Wipe. Spread."

"Hmm." Kari nodded and smiled. "I like that." She put her brush in the can and gave it a go. "Dip. Wipe. Spread. Nice!" She hesitated. "How do you feel today? About the move?"

"When the painting's done"—Ashley looked toward the driveway—"I might jump on the truck and head back home with the movers."

"You should stay." Kari sounded concerned. She kept painting.

Ashley painted another strip. "Maybe."

Get your copy of

Finding Home

by Karen Kingsbury and Tyler Russell
to finish the rest of the story!